W9-BHW-448

GET ALL THIS FREE
WITH JUST ONE PROOF OF PURCHASE:

$50 VALUE

◆ **Hotel Discounts** up to 60% at home and abroad ◆ **Travel Service** - Guaranteed lowest published airfares plus 5% cash back on tickets ◆ **$25 Travel Voucher** ◆ **Sensuous Petite Parfumerie** collection ◆ **Insider Tips Letter** with sneak previews of upcoming books

You'll get a FREE personal card, too. It's your passport to all these benefits—and to even more great gifts & benefits to come!

There's no club to join. No purchase commitment. No obligation.

HP-PP6A

Enrollment Form

☐ *Yes!* I WANT TO BE A *Privileged Woman*.
Enclosed is one *PAGES & PRIVILEGES*™ Proof of
Purchase from any Harlequin or Silhouette book currently for
sale in stores (Proofs of Purchase are found on the back pages
of books) and the store cash register receipt. Please enroll me
in *PAGES & PRIVILEGES*™. Send my Welcome Kit and FREE
Gifts -- and activate my FREE benefits -- immediately.

More great gifts and benefits to come.

NAME (please print)

ADDRESS   APT. NO

CITY   STATE   ZIP/POSTAL CODE

PROOF OF PURCHASE ONLY

**NO CLUB!
NO COMMITMENT!**
*Just one purchase brings
you great Free Gifts and
Benefits!*

Please allow 6-8 weeks for delivery. Quantities are limited. We reserve the right to
substitute items. Enroll before October 31, 1995 and receive one full year of benefits.

Name of store where this book was purchased_____

Date of purchase_____

Type of store:
☐ Bookstore   ☐ Supermarket   ☐ Drugstore
☐ Dept. or discount store (e.g. K-Mart or Walmart)
☐ Other (specify)_____

Which Harlequin or Silhouette series do you usually read?

_____

Complete and mail with one Proof of Purchase and store receipt to:
U.S.: *PAGES & PRIVILEGES*™, P.O. Box 1960, Danbury, CT 06813-1960
Canada: *PAGES & PRIVILEGES*™, 49-6A The Donway West, P.O. 813,
North York, ON M3C 2E8

HP-PP6B

"I don't understand you,"

Damian groaned softly against her compliant mouth. "I've tried to, but I can't. All I know is that I want you as I've never wanted anyone in my life before. Ros, I—"

"It doesn't matter," she whispered, silencing his tortured outburst with the melting tenderness of her own kiss.

She could use whatever ploy she wanted to occupy her mind, but she would never escape the fact that this was the man she loved, and if he needed her—no matter that it be a need in which love played no part— she would answer him and no power on earth would stop her.

KATE PROCTOR is part Irish and part Welsh, though she spent most of her childhood in England and several years of her adult life in Central Africa. She lives just outside London with her two cats, Florence and Minnie, presented to her by her two daughters who live fairly close by. Having given up her career as a teacher on her return to England, Kate now devotes most of her time to writing. Her hobbies include crossword puzzles, bridge and, at the moment, learning Spanish.

Books by Kate Proctor

Kate Proctor

Prince of Darkness

Harlequin Books

TORONTO • NEW YORK • LONDON
AMSTERDAM • PARIS • SYDNEY • HAMBURG
STOCKHOLM • ATHENS • TOKYO • MILAN
MADRID • WARSAW • BUDAPEST • AUCKLAND

ISBN 0-373-11767-1

PRINCE OF DARKNESS

First North American Publication 1995.

Copyright © 1992 by Kate Proctor.

CHAPTER ONE

THE knuckles of Rosanne Bryant's hands gleamed white against the dark leather of the steering-wheel as her yellow Mini snaked its way up the long, oak-lined drive towards Sheridan Hall. It was a wide and breath-takingly beautiful drive, but its beauty was lost on Rosanne, whose normally full-lipped mouth was tightened into a grim line as her mind relentlessly rehearsed her. Her name was Ros Grant, she chanted silently to herself: she had answered to the name Grant for the best part of her life— and shortening her first name shouldn't present too much of a problem, however unused she might be to it.

A long, shuddering sigh escaped her. She was almost there, but all she wanted to do was turn the car and head for anywhere other than the place now looming up ahead of her.

She shook her head, a look of bleak desolation marring the creamy oval of her face and filling the blue of her wide-spaced eyes with a depth of agony way beyond her twenty-four years. She would go on no matter what, she vowed grimly. She owed it to so many to do so: to the parents she had never known, to her paternal grandfather Edward Bryant, but perhaps most of all to herself.

It had been her grandpa Ted who had opened up the options for her that would one day lead her precisely here . . . but only if she herself made the choice. And she *had* made the choice, and now there could be no going back, she reminded herself, leaping out of the car before

the sudden rush of panic she was now experiencing en-
gulfed her entirely.

Her expression like that of one in a hypnotic trance,
she gazed around, the wintry paleness of the March sun-
light bringing the gleam of burnished copper to the
wayward curliness of her short-bobbed hair.

Three storeys high and with gabled attic windows
above them, there was little she sensed inviting in her
first impressions of Sheridan Hall, despite the softening
effect of the ivy masking most of the stern bleakness of
its glittering granite façade. She gave a small shiver, half
convinced that she was seeing a gleam of malevolence
emanating from the windows peering down through the
ivy-clad frames at her like watchful, waiting eyes.

'May I help you?'

Only just managing to suppress a shriek of pure terror,
Rosanne spun round and found the tall figure of a man
striding towards her. He was a truly magnificent
specimen of manhood, in his black polo-necked sweater,
cream riding breeches and gleaming brown leather boots.

'I beg your pardon?' stalled Rosanne, the debilitating
tension already hampering her now tightening to a point
where the ability to reason seemed to desert her completely. The man approaching her seemed, to her stu-
pefied mind, like a timeless apparition. Tall and perfectly
proportioned, his hair thick and inky-black and his eyes
the piercing blue of ice, his features so flawlessly
handsome that they might have been sculpted from
marble; and as he strode to a halt before her, his eyes
cool in their enquiry, she felt for all the world as though
she were trespassing in the realms of the Celtic princes
of old.

'I said—may I help you?' he repeated, his cultured
tone imperious despite the deceptive softness of its attractive Irish accent.

'I'm Ros Grant,' she stated, astounded to find that, despite the state she was in, she had actually remembered to abbreviate her name. 'I've come to see Mrs Cranleigh—in fact, to stay here.' She felt a peculiar tightening sensation in her chest as she wondered if this princely apparition could possibly be Damian Sheridan. If he was, she was face to face with only the second of her relatives—even though one only some sort of cousin umpteen times removed—she had met in her entire twenty-four years. 'She is expecting me,' she added with faltering confidence, as the man towering before her glared down at her for several seconds before speaking.

'To stay here?' he enquired, the sudden arching of his dark, boldly defined brows openly challenging her claim.

Rosanne's heart plummeted dejectedly. It had taken all the courage she possessed to get herself this far—the last thing she now needed was a hurdle of any description.

'I think you must have made a mistake,' he informed her with glacial politeness. 'Hester—Mrs Cranleigh—has mentioned nothing about expecting a guest.'

'But I'm from Bryant Publishing,' she protested, and instantly wished she had managed to sound at least a little assertive. 'Mrs Cranleigh has been in correspondence with us for some time now and specifically invited me here to help with preparations for her late husband's biography.'

His reaction—a string of torrid oaths muttered partially beneath his breath—threw her completely.

'I'm sorry!' he exclaimed, no hint of apology in the dazzling blue of the eyes now glowering darkly down at her, and promptly uttered another oath.

Having all but decided that turning and fleeing was the only option open to her, Rosanne hesitated as the man before her moved and, with a gesture of total exasperation, dragged his fingers through his hair—hair so many shades darker than her own, she found herself observing, yet with a tousled hint of curl quite similar to her own, she reasoned fancifully.

'Look— I really am sorry, Miss... what did you say your name was?'

'Grant—Ros Grant.'

He reached out a hand. 'Damian Sheridan.'

Her hand seemed to become lost in the tanned hugeness of his and her senses scattered as she became bathed in the dazzling brilliance of his unexpected smile.

Her feelings when she had first met Grandpa Ted had overwhelmed her too, she reminded herself shakily—but in a way not quite the same as this... and this man was so distant a relative that it scarcely counted.

'It's just that Mrs Cranleigh doesn't enjoy good health,' he said in that lovely, drawly voice that she was finding incredibly attractive.

'Mrs Cranleigh has been very frank with us about the state of her health,' replied Rosanne, once again experiencing that indefinable feeling she had had on first learning that the woman who was her maternal grandmother was probably terminally ill. 'And she cited that as one of the reasons she wanted me here as soon as possible.'

'Damn it—no doubt to sift through a few million of the fifty-odd million bits of paper that old devil stashed away!' exploded Damian Sheridan. 'The man seems to have kept old bus tickets, for God's sake!'

'But he was also a highly respected public figure in England and, I believe, here in Ireland,' stated Rosanne woodenly, confused to feel satisfaction rippling through her on discovering that this man was obviously not one of the legions worshipping the memory of the late politician-cum-philanthropist-cum-uncanonised saint that her late maternal grandfather was generally regarded as being.

'George Cranleigh was, at best, a sanctimonious prig,' snapped Damian Sheridan, with the candour of one plainly not given to mincing his words. 'Of course people here, and those over in England, regarded him as a great man—he used his wealth to make damned sure they did!'

'But that doesn't alter the fact that his widow wants his biography written—nor that I've been sent here to give her assistance to that effect,' pointed out Rosanne, while noting that this carelessly self-assured and outspoken man would, had circumstances been different, have been one whose brain she would have given her right arm to pick, despite the fact that he could only be in his very early thirties at the most.

'I doubt it's what she wants,' he retorted with open bitterness. 'It's what he demanded of her.' There was a look that was almost pleading softening a little of the arrogance from his compelling features. 'It's been over four years since he died and she's put it off all that time... now it's as though she sees it as her last duty to be carried out before she herself dies.'

Feeling herself falter in the face of such genuine concern, Rosanne found herself having to dredge up the savage hatred normally so ready to gnaw at her whenever the name Cranleigh entered her thoughts.

The gentle loveliness of her face tightened briefly to bitter harshness. 'Mr Sheridan, I have a job to do and I intend doing it. And don't you think you're being a touch melodramatic?'

'Melodrama's the engine that pumps Irish blood—or didn't you know that, darling?' he drawled sarcastically. 'I take it you have bags?' he added, frowning impatiently as Rosanne took some time responding, distracted by the realisation that some of that same blood, to which he had so bitingly referred, no doubt pumped in her own veins—albeit vastly diluted.

'They're in the boot,' she muttered, turning abruptly towards the car as she felt the colour rush to her cheeks.

He lifted her two bags from the boot, shaking his head as she made to remove the case containing her word processor.

'I'll send someone out for that.'

'I'm quite capable of carrying it for myself,' she protested.

'But you won't,' he informed her coolly. 'You see, liberation hasn't yet come to the women on my estates— so accept the fact that here you'll be waited on hand and foot.'

Her cheeks now stained with patches of scarlet, Rosanne followed his tall, broad-shouldered figure, empty-handed, to the vast, iron-studded front door— which he immediately kicked open with one elegantly booted foot. She had no idea whether or not he had been joking, but something warned her that this was one Irishman all too capable of using his gift with words to wound rather than to charm.

'James, get the rest of Miss Grant's things from the car, will you?' he muttered to the elderly retainer now appearing in the doorway. 'And try not to drop that case—it's no doubt filled with a load of high-falutin gear the likes of us would never understand,' he added with a careless chuckle.

'Bridie's got the lavender room ready for the wee girl,' James called over his shoulder as he tramped somewhat arthritically towards the car.

'Seem's as if I was wrong—you are expected,' shrugged Damian, striding across the gleaming wood of the huge galleried hallway and up its massive central staircase.

Quickening her steps in order to keep pace, Rosanne followed him up the thickly carpeted stairs. The place was enormous, she thought, feeling thoroughly over-whelmed, yet it gleamed with the attention so obviously

lavished on it...and the money too so obviously lavished on it, she decided as her feet seemed to float on
the extravagant pile of the sandy-coloured carpeting beneath them.

He took the right branch where the central staircase
divided in two, leading her down a wide corridor, along
the walls of which hung innumerable portraits. She
quickly averted her eyes from those sombre, oil-painted
faces peering down at her from their huge gilt frames,
then immediately began berating herself for being so
foolish. She had to draw a line somewhere! If these were
indeed his ancestors, they weren't necessarily any he had
in common with her.

'This is it,' he announced, depositing one of her bags
at his feet to enable him to open the door outside which
he had halted.

Rosanne found herself having to bite back a gasp of
pleasure as she stepped in. It was a huge, high-ceilinged
room and exquisitely furnished—and less like anything
she would describe as merely a bedroom than she had
ever seen, despite the large, canopied bed to the left of
it.

'Why on earth is it called the lavender room?' she
asked, unable to prevent her pleasure at the sight of her
white and gold surroundings from entering her tone.

'Ah, yes—I'm glad you asked,' murmured her companion, amusement dancing in his eyes. 'I used to ask
similar questions about this and other rooms when I was
a child—and never really did get a satisfactory answer.'

'Perhaps lavender was its original colour,' offered
Rosanne, oblivious of the spontaneous smile suddenly
softening the grave beauty of her face.

'Heaven help us—there's a brain beneath the beauty,'
murmured Damian Sheridan, his eyes flickering over her
slim body in a manner she found deflatingly non-

committal given his casually fulsome reference to her looks.

Disconcerted, she turned her back on both him and the bed, her eyes wary as they surveyed the rest of the room. There was a welcoming fire blazing in the grate beneath a gold and marble mantelpiece, and before it, cosily arranged on either side of a low, beautifully carved rectangular table, were two dainty yet invitingly comfortable-looking armchairs. The writing-bureau in the far corner, to the right of the second of two huge, three-quarter-length windows, was of the same pale, intricately carved wood as the table. As she stood there gazing around her she was aware of a curious reluctance within her to accept how much she liked what she was seeing—not just the beauty and the exquisite taste surrounding her, but the actual *feel* of it all.

'The door to the left of the bed leads to the dressing-room,' muttered Damian Sheridan, 'and the one on the right to the bathroom.' He turned at the sound of a knock on the door and opened it to the elderly retainer. 'James, what possessed you to carry that thing up all those stairs?' he demanded exasperatedly, relieving the man of the case holding Rosanne's word processor.

'Damian, would you stop fussing?' muttered the man irritably. 'You're getting worse than Bridie!'

Rosanne turned, desperate to hide her amusement as her own murmured thanks were greeted by an almost baleful look. There was a lot more to the arrogant and aristocratic Damian Sheridan than first met the eye, she was deciding. Not only did his staff, or at least the elderly James, call him by his first name—but he didn't seem to object in the least to a bit of plain speaking, which James was now giving him in plenty by the door.

'And you want to do something about Joe,' James was grumbling. 'Have you seen what the lad's doing to your grass with yon horse?'

Damian Sheridan strode towards the window furthest from her, letting out a string of audibly ripe oaths as he dragged up the lower half of the sash-window and seemed about to hurl himself out through it.

'Joe, would you get that damned animal off my lawn, for God's sake?' he roared.

Helplessly intrigued, Rosanne walked over to the second window, which she discovered looked out over a vast expanse of immaculately tended lawns that seemed to slope to the white-flecked turbulence of the sea beyond. Right below her on the lawn, she spotted what had to be the object of Damian Sheridan's wrath. He was a slim, wiry young man of around her own age, mounted on a plainly high-spirited small horse.

The young man was grinning up at the window.

'Just watch this, will you, Damian?' he called up pleadingly.

Rosanne leaned her head against the window-pane, trying frantically to stifle her laughter as, to the exasperated roar of the man hanging perilously out of the adjoining window, Joe turned the horse and raced it at startling speed right down the centre of the lawn. Then, turning at an impossibly tight angle, he raced the horse back to where they had started.

'Now tell me,' demanded Joe triumphantly, 'did you see any trace of lameness?'

'Not a trace,' chuckled the man at the window, his easy laughter confounding Rosanne—his beautiful lawn was virtually in ruins right down its centre! 'Give him another run in the sea—and get someone to see to that damned grass, before you end up lamed by Bridie!'

Still grinning proudly, the rider saluted and rode off.

Rosanne drew back from the second window as the first was slammed shut, information she had been given about Damian Sheridan, but which hadn't interested her in the least at the time, now returning to her.

'I hear you breed polo ponies,' she stated as he approached her and remembered also hearing that he had been a top player himself until a bad accident had forced him to give up competitive play.

'Do you, now?' he drawled with not a trace of the warmth and laughter so evident in him scant seconds ago.

'When may I see Mrs Cranleigh?' asked Rosanne, determined not to be goaded into lowering herself to the level of his rudeness and ignoring his taunting words.

'Did you come here expecting one of those warm Irish welcomes you've no doubt heard about?' he enquired with soft malevolence, sauntering right up to her. 'Because if that's the case you're in for a big disappointment.'

'For your information, I also happen to have Irish blood in me—so you can drop that line of needling,' flashed Rosanne angrily, then immediately wondered what on earth had possessed her to come out with a claim like that, no matter what its technical truth. 'And I came here expecting absolutely nothing of you, Mr Sheridan,' she added, anger still blazing in the eyes meeting his despite the calmness she had managed to inject into her tone. 'I've already told you, I——'

'Yes, as you say, you've already told me,' he interrupted brusquely, then strode past her and flung himself down on one of the deceptively dainty armchairs—most deceptively dainty in that it didn't, as Rosanne had half hoped, collapse beneath him. 'Come over here and sit down,' he ordered abruptly. 'We need to talk.'

If ever there was a time for her to cut her losses and run, this was it, she told herself desperately, but her legs were already carrying her towards the second chair and by the time she had sat down she knew that the opportunity was gone forever.

'Mr Sheridan——'

'Damian.'

'All right—Damian,' agreed Rosanne—then racked her brains for what it was she had been about to say. 'You wanted to talk,' she added for want of remembering.

Whatever its deceptive strength, the armchair into which he had flung himself was far too small to accommodate a man his size. He hunched his broad shoulders slightly, easing his body down as he lifted his booted feet and plonked them, ankles crossed, on the low table between them. There was no shred of friendliness in the dark—now almost navy—blue of the eyes regarding her.

'Bryant Publishing—how long have you been with them?' he demanded.

It took all the control she possessed for Rosanne not to flinch from the total unexpectedness of that question— nor the others it instantly conjured up within her.

'Six months,' she replied, with no trace of the turmoil stirring within. It was six months since Grandpa Ted had died and left her all he possessed, part of which had been a fifty per cent share in Bryant Publishing.

'The name rang a vague bell in me when you mentioned it earlier,' stated Damian pensively. 'It's just now occurred to me why.'

Rosanne forced her features into an expression of polite interest while her mind churned frantically. When, some months before her grandfather's death, Hester Cranleigh had put her first tentative feelers out to Bryant's regarding the biography, Rosanne had been stunned, to put it mildly.

'It's futile to try to guess why,' her grandfather had said. 'It's up to you alone whether you choose to seek the answer.'

'I didn't like it when Hester first started on it,' Damian was muttering as though to himself, 'and now I'm liking it even less.' His eyes flashed accusation into hers. 'I suppose you regard this as simply another job and that it wouldn't occur to you that there are a number of hornets' nests this sort of thing will disturb.'

'I'm sure any widow contemplating her late husband's biography is aware that memories both good and bad are bound to be revived,' replied Rosanne. She had felt no need for answers when Grandpa Ted was alive, but now he was gone there was a desperate yearning in her for them—all of them!

'Believe you me, I doubt if many of them will be good,' he retorted with a harsh laugh, raising his hands behind him and gripping the back of the chair. 'Are you aware that Hester had a daughter?' he demanded.

She had done all she could to prepare herself for this, the first mention of her own mother, sensing that it could possibly be her most testing. But nothing could have prepared her for this indescribable mixture of fear and exhilaration tearing through her.

'Yes, I know that the Cranleighs had a daughter—and that she died tragically young,' she stated, her words controlled and almost expressionless.

'Faith was barely nineteen when she died,' muttered Damian. 'She ran off with the lad she was in love with—only for the pair of them to be killed in a plane crash on the way to some far-flung refuge or other.'

Kenya, filled in Rosanne silently: the Bryants had had a property there, which was to have been her parents' haven.

'Why...?' She gave a small cough, trying to clear the sudden distorted croak from her voice. 'You say they ran off...' The words petered to a halt, alarming her. If she was in danger of losing control at this early stage it was pointless even attempting to go on.

'Apparently the saintly George wasn't happy with his daughter's choice of man,' explained Damian, anger and disgust in his tone. 'So the poor girl had no choice but to run. George Cranleigh was a man who liked to have his own way—no matter what it cost.'

Rosanne felt her head begin to swim; could Damian Sheridan possibly know? His hatred for George Cranleigh seemed almost to match her own, though his, unlike hers, most certainly didn't encompass George's widow.

'You hated him, didn't you?' she heard herself say.

'Did I?' he asked with a shrug. 'They still talk of Hester Sheridan around here. They talk of her as one of the most beautiful and vivacious women in all Ireland...as she was when she met and married her dour English politician.' He gave a harsh laugh. 'They say she worked wonders on him—that some of her sparkle rubbed off on him and enhanced his political stature.' He shrugged, as though doubting even that claim. 'They came here often; Hester had spent a lot of time in this house as a child and regarded it as her home. I remember those visits from when I was a very small child...that is to say, I remember Hester—he seemed no more than a dark shadow.' He glanced across at her, the ice in his eyes reaching out to chill her. 'I couldn't have been more than about eight when Faith and her young man were killed in that crash, but I was old enough to sense how much of Hester had died with them when she came back here.'

Rosanne felt her hands clench in her lap as she fought back the helpless rage threatening to burst from her. Why should anything of Hester Cranleigh have died with the daughter and son-in-law she and her husband had so cruelly deceived? Damian had referred to her father as Faith's 'young man', yet he was the husband she had defied her parents by running away to marry when she was only seventeen. And he was the man she had gone on loving even when her father had used his position to have them separated and her made a ward of court.

Hester and George Cranleigh had lost their daughter long before the tragedy that had killed her . . . but at least they had known her, protested Rosanne in silent torment. Grandpa Ted had broken down and wept when he had told her of the heartrending grief suffered by his son Paul and his daughter-in-law Faith that their daughter, conceived in such joyous love, had been stillborn during their terrible months of separation.

Rosanne leapt to her feet, certain that she would betray herself if she didn't allow herself the distraction of movement.

'That's all very sad,' she stated tonelessly, walking to the nearest window and gazing sightlessly out through it, 'but it really has no bearing on the fact that Mrs Cranleigh——'

'You're a cold-hearted little bitch, aren't you?' demanded Damian Sheridan, beside her before she was even conscious of his having moved and grasping her painfully by the shoulders to swing her round to face the scowling darkness of his features. 'I'm nowhere near finished with what I have to say. Hester Cranleigh is one of the most decent women I've ever known and she has remained so despite all the dirt life has thrown up at her! I was fifteen when my parents were killed in a road accident, and it was Hester who returned here to live so that there would be a loving home for me to come back to during my school holidays and later from university. It was Hester who did all in her power to help fill the gap left by my parents' death. And it's Hester I'll protect from any more hurt with my last breath, if needs be!'

Rosanne's eyes dropped from the fury blazing in his. She had spent so long psyching herself up for this . . . yet now she was here she was encountering obstacles she could never have envisaged. She would do everything in her power to hurt the woman who had deprived Faith and Paul of even knowing of the existence of the daughter they had so mourned; and for depriving her paternal grandmother of the granddaughter she would have adored; and, most of all, for having cheated Grandpa Ted of all but two years of the life of the granddaughter for whom his unstinting love had been like the elixir of life. And for that, she was certain, this beautiful, passionate Irishman would do all in his power to destroy her.

'Has it never occurred to you that she might not want this protection you so threateningly offer?' asked Rosanne quietly. 'After all, undertaking this biography was Mrs Cranleigh's choice ultimately, despite it having been her husband's wish. And she must know better than anyone what the research will entail emotionally.'

His hands dropped from her shoulders, then he took a step nearer the window and rested his forehead against the glass.

'Paul Bryant—that was the name of the man Faith ran away with,' he muttered hoarsely.

The man she had married almost two years previously, Rosanne wanted to cry out to him.

'So why, of all places, would Hester choose a publishing company of that same name?'

'Perhaps *because* of that name...I just wouldn't know,' replied Rosanne. Grandpa Ted had never shown any animosity towards Hester, but neither had he shown any desire to contact her—the decision as to whether or not to delve into the darkness of Rosanne's maternal roots was one he had made plain was hers and hers alone. But one thing she now remembered so vividly was how her grandfather's bitterness and loathing had always been concentrated solely on George Cranleigh.

'Perhaps!' he exclaimed with harsh bitterness, turning from the window and facing her. 'I'm wasting my breath trying to change your mind, aren't I?'

'Yes, you are.'

His eyes flickered over her slim figure with cold distaste.

'You realise, don't you, that, this being my property, I can have you slung off it whenever I choose?'

'And I suppose you choose now,' stated Rosanne, refusing to acknowledge that her immediate reaction, if it came to that, would be one of colossal relief.

'No—as it happens—I don't choose now,' he drawled, his look now one of deliberate offensiveness as his eyes lazily perused her body. 'As long as you agree to my conditions.'

'It depends what they are,' replied Rosanne, colour rising treacherously in her cheeks as she wondered what she would do if the blatant sensuality of the message in his eyes had any bearing on those conditions.

'Hester's grown quite weak of late and she's virtually bedridden now—so you'll be working very much on your own,' he stated brusquely, blanking the heat from his eyes. 'I take it that your job here is to sift through the papers for relevant material?'

Rosanne nodded, feeling edgy and uncertain. Perhaps the strain was getting to her already...perhaps she had only imagined that arrogant sexuality in his eyes.

'But it'll be Hester sifting through your findings to decide what really is pertinent,' he continued.

Again Rosanne nodded.

'You will report to me, on a daily basis, with all your findings in clear note form...and you will do so before you have any contact with Hester regarding your day's work.'

'You think I'm likely to unearth things——'

'What I think is immaterial,' he interrupted impatiently. 'Do you agree—or do you leave?'

'Obviously I have no choice if I'm to do my job,' she retorted angrily.

'With a brain as quick as yours you'll go far, Ros,' he murmured sarcastically. 'What's that short for—Rosamund?'

Rosanne eyed him warily, then shrugged non-committally.

'Rosamund—it doesn't suit you in the least,' he murmured, suddenly giving her a smile that seemed to reach out and warm her with its dazzling brilliance.

'That's why I prefer Ros,' she muttered, conscious of the colour rising yet again in her cheeks. For whatever reason, and she couldn't for the life of her even begin to guess why, Damian Sheridan had decided to switch on the charm. The fact that her every sense was responding to that charm as though plugged into high-voltage electricity was something she found profoundly disturbing...which only went to show the terrible tension she was under, she reasoned with edgy uncertainty.

'Ros,' he murmured, almost caressingly, then tilted his head to one side, frowning slightly. 'It's funny, but suddenly you remind me of someone.' He reached out, taking her chin in his hand and angling her face towards the light from the window. 'I can't think who, just now...but it'll come to me.'

'When will I be able to see Mrs Cranleigh?' asked Rosanne hoarsely, her beleaguered mind unable to decide which was having a more devastating affect on her—his troubling words or his equally disturbing touch.

'When she's feeling up to it, she likes to have tea in the blue drawing-room...the one that's now green,' he murmured, his hand a charged warmth against her skin.

She was still trying to decide whether she would only make a complete fool of herself by asking him to remove his hand when he pulled her against him with a swiftness that left her mind still grappling with the problem of his hand. And her mind was still several steps behind when he lowered his head to hers and kissed her. It was a kiss not only completely unexpected, but one so electrifyingly exciting, so disconcertingly assured of its welcome, that her lips momentarily parted, not so much in acquiescence, but with eager spontaneity to the demands of the mouth coaxing them open with practised ease.

It was the movement of her own hands, spreading for no other reason than to revel in the solid expanse of chest beneath them, that sent a jolt of confounded awareness through her.

It brought her little comfort that, the instant her hands began pushing against him in protest, he immediately released her. And it brought her even less comfort to hear the soft rumble of laughter growling from deep within him as she let out a belated gasp of outrage.

'For a while there I'd thought I'd found a woman with guts enough to say, "To hell" and give in to her instincts,' he chuckled.

'If you so much as lay one finger on me again, I *shall* give in to my instincts,' retorted Rosanne hoarsely, her eyes dropping in utter mortification from the mocking amusement in his. 'Which tell me to slap your face,' she added furiously.

'Liar,' he laughed with lazy self-assurance. 'Tell me, Ros—are you absolutely sure you won't change your mind about staying?'

'Absolutely,' she spat, her cheeks crimson.

'Well, if that's the case, we really should consider moving your things into my room—because that's the place those irresistible instincts of yours will sooner or later lead you.'

CHAPTER TWO

IT WAS turning into a complete nightmare, thought Rosanne frantically, her eyes refusing to meet the mockery gleaming openly in those of Damian Sheridan as he held open the door of the blue drawing-room... the one that was in fact green. And it was a nightmare that was completely self-inflicted, she reproached herself futilely as she forced her reluctant legs forward.

For two years, the most intensely happy in her entire life, she had been a whole and contented person, cocooned in the love so unstintingly lavished on her by her grandfather. And it had been a mutual love, so sure and safe in its joyous strength that even her gradual learning of the cruel treachery perpetrated on her in the past had been powerless to taint it with its evil darkness.

'I'm an old man who has received the most precious jewel—one he never dreamed was rightfully his,' he had told her. 'Yet when I first learned of your existence I was like a madman, filled with a murderous need for revenge on those who had perpetrated this monstrous evil. And, God forgive me, had George Cranleigh been alive that day, I think I could have killed him with my bare hands.' Even the embers of that hatred, flashing momentarily in his eyes as he had spoken, had been awesome. 'But the instant I found you love freed me from that destructive hatred...can you understand that, my darling child?'

Oh, how she had understood, cherishing each precious moment of those glorious months into which they had crammed a lifetime of loving. But even the powerful

23

legacy of that love he had lavished on her had been unable to prevent the anger and bitterness rampaging alongside her anguish once he had gone—just as he had always tried to warn her it would. And, because he had foreseen the need that would one day drive her, he had done all he could to ease her way along the hazardous path that would eventually lead her here.

And here, she told herself, her heart pounding, was to this exquisitely elegant room in delicate greens and to the frail, bird-like woman almost lost in the moss-green hugeness of a fan-backed velvet chair...and to feelings akin to terror.

'Miss Ros Grant to see you, Hester,' teased Damian, striding over to the tiny woman and kissing her up-turned cheek. 'I know how you hate abbreviated names, but I'm afraid Ros is all she'll answer to.'

Ros, an anguished voice cried out inside her, because Rosanne was a name she dared not utter—the name her mother had vowed to give a daughter if she ever had one.

'Stop prattling, Damian,' scolded Hester Cranleigh affectionately, 'and bring her over here so that I can see her.'

As Damian beckoned her, Rosanne took several steps forward, her knees like jelly, her eyes lowered from the woman they could not bring themselves to examine.

'Good gracious!' exclaimed Hester Cranleigh, her words freezing the now terrified girl.

Grandpa Ted had told her that it was because she was such a perfect blend of her mother and father that her likeness to either one wouldn't immediately strike anyone who had known them...but that had been Grandpa Ted's opinion.

'You're just a child!' exclaimed the old lady. 'I was expecting someone a lot older.'

'But I'm twenty-four... I mean, twenty-five,' stammered Rosanne, almost collapsing with relief.

'Any advance on twenty-five?' drawled Damian, his look taunting.

'I keep forgetting,' muttered Rosanne. 'You see, I've only recently had a birthday.' Her twenty-fourth, she reminded herself angrily—unnecessary lies were bound to tie her up in knots. She *had* to get a grip on herself!

'Damian, stop browbeating the poor child,' chided Hester, smiling sympathetically up at Rosanne, 'and draw up a chair for her—nice and close to me.'

Damian did as requested then, as Rosanne gingerly sat down, flung himself full-length on the sofa beside them, linking his hands behind his head as he gazed over at the two women.

'You'd better be Mother, Ros,' he said, indicating the laden tea-trolley beside him. 'I tend to be accident-prone around china.'

'Damian tends to be accident-prone around anything he doesn't feel like doing,' murmured Hester drily, flashing Rosanne a warmly conspiratorial look that had the effect of freezing the blood in her veins. 'Darling, haven't you some horses or something to attend to?' she enquired pointedly of the supine man.

'No,' he replied uncooperatively, flashing her one of his megawatt smiles.

'Damian, I won't have you being difficult,' warned Hester with a sigh. 'And I'm sure you know perfectly well why Ros is here.'

'Oh, I do, darling,' he murmured. 'I had to horsewhip the information out of her—since you omitted to tell me we were expecting her. And, to make things even simpler, I've let her know exactly how I feel about all this—so we've absolutely nothing to hide.' He rose to his feet, his movements languidly graceful, then smiled cherubically. 'And just this once I'll be Mother,' he said, then added, 'though another point I felt it only fair to warn our guest about is my feudal attitude to women.'

Hester Cranleigh's eyes twinkled as they met Rosanne's.

'And just you keep that warning in mind, my dear,' she whispered, loud enough for the man she plainly adored to catch. 'I'd like to be able to tell you it's because of his scandalous behaviour towards you girls that he's still a single man at almost thirty-two, but I'm afraid I can't. Despite the appalling way he treats them, the poor fools queue up in their droves to have their hearts broken. I do so hope you don't turn out to be one such fool, my dear,' she murmured, then startled an almost paralysed Rosanne into shocked awareness by winking broadly at her.

'Now who's prattling?' demanded Damian with an unconcerned smile, placing a tray on her lap.

'Thank you, darling,' murmured the old lady, smiling up at him. 'And, by the way, I was thinking it would be rather nice to have the Blakes over for dinner again soon.'

Damian's reaction was to scowl blackly at her, then return to the tea-trolley.

'Gerry Blake is Damian's vet—such a nice man,' murmured Hester. 'And his daughter Nerissa——'

'What do you take in your tea?' cut in Damian rudely, addressing Rosanne. 'Or perhaps you'd rather pour it for yourself?'

'I'd pour it myself, if I were you, my dear,' murmured Hester, raising a slice of cake to her mouth. 'He's slopped mine in the saucer.'

Rosanne rose, in the thrall of a terrible sense of unreality as she poured herself some tea. Reason had always warned her it was impossible to prepare herself for this—especially for what sort of person her grandmother might turn out to be. But what now confused and distressed her was the realisation that, in different circumstances, she could have so easily fallen under the spell of this outgoing and, to be completely honest, delightfully humorous old lady.

'You might as well pour me one while you're up,' muttered Damian, once more sprawled along the length of the sofa.

Rosanne hesitated, strongly tempted to tell him to pour his own.

'Well, well,' chuckled the old lady delightedly. 'It seems as though Ros is actually contemplating not complying with that graciously worded request of yours, my lad. Nerissa Blake, on the other hand, would already be pouring you your second cup.'

Startled to find herself having difficulty keeping her face straight, Rosanne poured him a cup and took it to him.

'And Nerissa would have put a level spoon of sugar in it for me,' he complained, laughter glinting in his eyes.

'And no doubt stirred it for him too,' murmured Hester, when Rosanne presented him with the sugar bowl.

'What about some cake?' he demanded.

'Thanks, I'd love some,' replied Rosanne, cutting herself a slice of the tempting Madeira and returning to her seat.

'Could it be that you've at last met your match, my fine young heart-breaker?' chortled Hester, her eyes twinkling as he rose disgruntledly and got himself some cake.

'I doubt it, darling,' he murmured, his eyes suddenly catching Rosanne's and bringing hot colour flooding to her cheeks with their taunting challenge. 'I doubt it very much.'

'Well, that remains to be seen,' muttered Hester, plainly sensing the sudden tension. 'Anyway, Ros,' she continued brightly, 'tell me all about yourself. You'll be delving into my life, during the next weeks, as few others have, so I feel it only fair that I should be allowed a little delving of my own to even things up a bit.'

Desperately playing for time in which to gather her once again hopelessly scattered wits, Rosanne took a mouthful of cake. She had expected to be asked a few personal questions and had prepared herself for them... but this disarming demand for her life history was the last thing she was prepared for.

Lies were out, she warned herself frantically, remembering the fairly innocuous lie she had told about her age, and her fears that it would rebound on her.

'There's not a lot to tell,' she muttered uncomfortably as she swallowed the last of her mouthful. All she could do was stick with the truth as far as possible.

'You'd be amazed by what Hester can extract from even the most apparently humdrum of lives,' stated Damian, the narrowed shrewdness of his watching eyes terrifying her.

'Don't be so rude, Damian,' Hester rebuked him. 'Ros has a very interesting job and I'm sure her family is very proud of her.'

'Hester, you might think it's interesting to plough through George's bits and pieces,' he drawled. 'Frankly, I'd get more of a thrill mucking out stables.'

'Well, you're not Ros,' snapped Hester, looking slightly shocked. 'And I'm sure your people are very proud of you, and rightly so,' she added, smiling apologetically at Rosanne.

'I haven't got any people,' blurted out Rosanne before she could stop herself. 'I mean...I...my grandfather died last year.'

She wanted to leap to her feet and run—to escape this ordeal and to leave behind this stricken, inarticulate creature who had taken her over and was making her sound such a fool.

'My dear, how sad!' exclaimed Hester Cranleigh, reaching out a frail hand to her in reflex sympathy. 'Was he all the family you had?'

'Yes—he was,' said Rosanne, her body tensing with the effort it took not to flinch from the hand patting solicitously on her arm. How could this woman possibly care? she asked herself savagely as hatred, hot and harsh, seared through her. 'I was adopted when I was a baby, but my adoptive parents moved to Australia a few years ago.'

'Was it your real or adoptive grandfather who died?' asked Hester, removing her hand from Rosanne's arm as though conscious of its lack of welcome.

'He was my *real* grandfather,' replied Rosanne, an edge of desperation in her tone. 'The person I loved more than anyone else.'

'Damian, would you mind taking my tray, there's a dear?' murmured Hester, the sudden frailness in her voice inexplicably cooling the heat of hatred within Rosanne.

'I'm sorry,' she whispered, convinced that they must think her deranged, 'but I still find it difficult talking about my grandfather.'

'Of course you do, my dear,' sympathised Hester, as a granite-faced Damian towered above them and took the tray. 'And I'm sure that, missing him as you do, you find it hard to realise how lucky you were to have had him—most adopted children don't have a blood relative around to whom they can turn to ask all those questions that must inevitably crop up in their minds.'

There was an expression of dazed disbelief on Rosanne's face as she turned and looked at the small, frail figure seated beside her... How could she possibly have allowed herself to make such a statement with a secret as dark as hers festering inside her?

'Ros—would you like more tea?' Damian's tone was harsh as his words interrupted her reeling thoughts and his look, when she dazedly turned to face him, openly hostile.

'No—no, thank you,' she muttered, then addressed the woman beside her without looking at her. 'Believe me, I know exactly how lucky I was to have had my grandfather.'

'It's sad that you didn't get on with your adoptive parents,' stated Hester quietly.

'Now you're being fanciful, Hester,' teased Damian, while flashing Rosanne a scowling look. 'She said nothing about not getting on with them.'

'She didn't have to,' replied Hester, a questioning sadness in her eyes as they met Rosanne's.

Rosanne hesitated, feeling strangely compelled to answer that questioning look, her nervousness in the face of such a compulsion exacerbated by the almost threatening look to which Damian was subjecting her from the sofa.

'No—I didn't get on with them,' she eventually stated tonelessly. 'But now that I'm older I can see that much of the fault for that lay with me.'

It was her discussions with her grandfather about her life with John and Marjory Grant that had opened her eyes to that fact and had made her realise that the Grants' openness about her having been adopted had, in many ways, been her salvation. In a conservative, God-fearing household—with two much older natural daughters who were carbon copies of their parents—she would have stood out like a sore thumb anyway with her vibrant looks and fiery temper. But it was the sum of money for her future education that George Cranleigh had handed over together with his baby granddaughter that had set her so totally apart from the Grant family. From the age of six she had been sent to boarding-schools, as opposed to the local school the other two Grant girls attended, isolating her completely and compounding totally her sense of being the odd one out. In trying to salvage what faint conscience he might have had by providing for the future education of the baby granddaughter he had otherwise dumped as unwanted baggage, George Cranleigh had only ensured that she would always feel alienated and insecure.

'A bit of a rebel, were you?' asked Hester, her tone implying approval.

'Caused, no doubt, by that Irish blood she was telling me about earlier,' drawled Damian in tones that were neither approving nor in the least friendly. 'You're looking a little tired, Hester—how about another cup of tea?'

'No, thank you, darling,' replied the old lady. 'But perhaps Ros would now, to help wash down Bridie's cake.'

Rosanne flushed guiltily as she glanced at the piece of cake, on the small table beside her, out of which she had only managed a single bite—the nervous tension churning inside her making her feel almost nauseous.

'No, I shan't, thank you very much,' she said, reaching over and breaking off a small portion of the cake.

'Perhaps it's time we showed Ros George's study— where she'll be doing her work,' suggested Damian. 'Then we can get you tucked up for a rest,' he added gently. 'You look as though you could do with one.'

'I think it might be an even better idea for you to take me up now—then you can show Ros the study.' Hester turned to Rosanne, the exhaustion that had so swiftly overtaken her now etched plainly on her face. 'I do hope you'll forgive me, my dear. This wretched business of being an invalid can be such a nuisance. No—you stay there and relax,' she protested, as Ros made to rise to her feet. 'Damian will see me to my room,' she added, reaching for the stick propped against her chair as Damian rose and strode over to help her. 'And he'll show you around George's office and help you get settled in— or he'll have me to answer to,' she chuckled up at the man easing her to her feet.

'You'll have me quaking in my breeches if I don't,' he teased affectionately, slipping his arm around her as she leaned heavily on her stick.

'And that's another thing,' chided Hester, as they made their laborious way across the huge room. 'I'm not having you appear at the dinner table in your riding breeches—do you hear? Whatever will young Ros think of us?'

Their sparring remarks liberally interspersed with loving laughter, they made their slow progress towards the door—the stooped and fragile old lady and the tall, powerfully built, yet gracefully slender man against whose arm she leant.

They were part of her family—the family she had dreamed since childhood that she would one day find, thought Rosanne, the memory an ache within her that mirrored itself in the eyes that followed them.

But the Cranleighs had made certain she would find no one, she reminded herself bitterly. Paul and Faith Addison were the names entered as her parents on her birth certificate. She closed her eyes, reliving the rage of anguish that had been her grandfather's when he had seen that document.

'My God, not only was Cranleigh heartless, he also criminally falsified the records!' he had raged. 'Addison was your grandmother's maiden name—we gave it to Paul as his middle name. Dear God, how could anyone cut off an innocent child from her roots so brutally?'

It had always been George against whom Grandpa Ted's helpless rage had been directed...but he was a chivalrous old gentleman who would never speak ill of a woman, no matter what he might think of her. Yet now Rosanne found herself wondering if that really was the case. Her every instinct recoiled from the idea of Hester Cranleigh being involved in such cruel deception.

Wishful thinking would change nothing, she told herself harshly, her eyes opening to gaze down at the hands clenching and unclenching agitatedly in her lap. She was a Bryant and needed nothing from the Cranleighs, she reminded herself in an attempt to lessen the black despair engulfing her; she had had all the love, and more, she could ever have asked for from her darling grandfather.

'Hester won't be coming down for dinner this evening,' announced Damian, his face like a thunder-cloud as he strode across the room towards Rosanne. 'And that harrowing little orphan-Annie scenario to which you subjected her probably set her back months. Just what the hell do you think you're playing at?'

Rosanne leapt to her feet, her reason deserting her.

'How dare you speak to me like that?' she demanded hoarsely, resentment and loathing burning in her eyes. 'You know absolutely nothing about——' She broke off, her lips clamping tight with the horrified realisation of what she had been about to hurl at him in thoughtless rage.

'What is it I know nothing about?' he demanded, scowling down accusingly at her.

'Nothing—just forget it,' she muttered defeatedly. 'I came here to do a job, not to be harassed and shouted at by you—so just leave me alone!'

'One thing I have no intention of doing is leaving you alone, my unwelcome Ros,' he retorted with a grim travesty of a smile. 'Hester Cranleigh happens to be one of those exceptionally rare creatures among mankind— a generous, warm-hearted and indiscriminately loving person who would never knowingly do even her worst enemy harm. I'd move heaven and earth to ensure her last days are spent in relative peace—and the chances are I'll end up having to move both, given the memories this work on her husband's biography will inevitably resurrect. But what she doesn't need is harrowing tales of your ghastly childhood to——'

'I never said anything about having had a ghastly childhood,' cut in Rosanne indignantly. 'And I certainly don't go round telling harrowing tales about myself!'

'Well, they're harrowing to a woman who's been forced to relive her past and who could well have had a grandchild around your age, had her daughter not lost the baby. You prattling on about how wonderful your relationship was with your grandfather—how the hell do you think that must have made her feel?'

'And how was I supposed to know any of that?' demanded Rosanne, trembling with rage and disbelief. If only he knew, she kept asking herself, what would his reaction be?

'Well, you know now,' he snapped, his eyes dark and unyielding as they glared down into hers.

'What I do know is that you seem to have an extremely fertile imagination,' she informed him coldly. 'But you needn't worry because, as I tried to make clear earlier, I'm not given to talking about my private life to strangers, so Mrs Cranleigh won't be subjected to any voluntary disclosures from me that are likely to upset her.'

'And they sure as hell wouldn't be involuntary, would they, Ros?' he demanded harshly. 'It's only when you lose that so-called Irish temper of yours that you ever let anything slip, isn't that so?'

Rosanne tried to take a step back from the man towering accusingly above her and found her legs wedged against the edge of the chair.

'Yet when you're in control of yourself,' he continued ruthlessly, 'I get the feeling that not a single word passes those delightfully tempting lips of yours without having first been coldly weighed up and calculated.'

'As I said before—you have an extremely fertile imagination,' said Rosanne hoarsely. She had been here scant hours, she thought dazedly, and already she had been subjected to far more than she had ever dreamed she could take—and the vast majority of it from someone she had never even considered as a potential threat.

'Ah, so you deny you feel the world owes you something, do you?' he challenged softly.

'Why on earth do you think I feel that?' she protested, aghast.

'Because it's written all over you,' he replied. 'And I must say I find the idea of your becoming an embittered, shrivelled-up harridan most disturbing,' he added, placing his hands on her shoulders and drawing her towards him with a casual ease that stunned her into immobility.

'You do?' she croaked dazedly.

'Oh, I most certainly do, darling,' he chuckled, his hands sliding lightly down her arms. 'That's why I feel almost duty-bound to light that fire just begging to be lit inside you—and to do so before it's too late.'

'You mean before I become that shrivelled-up harridan you're so worried I'll turn into?' asked Rosanne, the scepticism she had intended not manifesting itself the least satisfactorily in her tone. He was being outrageous and they both knew it, but she desperately hoped that the disturbingly sensuous effect that his nearness and the teasing lightness of his touch were having on her was something of which she alone was aware.

'I was right—you do have a brain,' he murmured with an exaggerated sigh of contentment, then suddenly pulled her against the length of him.

'Well, you can't have much of a brain if you think I'm going to fall for a line as blatant as that,' she said, but her intended laugh deteriorated into a choked gasp as she quickly turned her head to avoid the confidently smiling mouth descending towards hers.

'You'd be surprised, the number of women who respond to that sort of drivel,' he murmured unabashedly, his lips sending disconcertingly sharp shocks of pleasure through her as they played against her cheek. 'And frankly, if I were a woman, I'd be inclined to use my fists on the likes of me,' he added with a chuckle, while his arms slid slowly around her.

'A thought something along those lines had just crossed my mind,' said Rosanne, appalled to hear breathless excitement instead of dismissive lightness in her tone. She was almost immediately distracted from that problem by yet another—the fact not so much that his mouth seemed to be making rapid progress towards hers, but that her every instinct now was to turn her head that fraction that would unite their mouths.

'You know, that's the second time today that a woman has had me quaking in my breeches,' he chuckled, his lips now nuzzling against hers with such electrifying effect that Rosanne was incapable of even considering whether or not she had accommodatingly moved her head. 'Oh, hell, that reminds me,' he sighed—a sigh that mingled their breaths in a way Rosanne was finding every bit as inflammatory as a full-blown kiss. 'Hester will skin me alive if I don't obey her orders.'

His abrupt release of her came so unexpectedly that for a moment he had to put out a hand to steady her.

There was a half-smile playing against his lips as he gazed down at her.

'Well, at least we got that problem sorted out,' he murmured. 'So now I'd better lead you to the great man's study.'

He turned and began strolling across the room.

'And what exactly was that problem we've allegedly just sorted out?' Rosanne called after him, a strange lightness—almost a feeling of frivolity—dancing through her.

He paused mid-stride, then spoke without turning. 'As you didn't use your fists on me this time—I'll not insult your intelligence the next time.'

The teasing softness of his laughter sent a shiver through her, a shiver that was anticipatory, yet almost as pleasurable as those she had experienced so sharply in those brief moments in his arms.

She was smiling as she began walking after him. Damian Sheridan as an enemy was a frighteningly daunting prospect, whereas Damian Sheridan in romantic pursuit of her...

His steps slowed as he reached the door, then he turned. The eyes that swept her from head to toe as she walked towards him were predatory eyes, dark with the promise of desires in which romance would play no part.

And the shiver that rippled through her, as he turned once again, was one suddenly filled with foreboding.

CHAPTER THREE

ROSANNE watched Damian as he read her day's notes, the unpalatable truth striking her that she actually looked forward to these daily meetings of theirs.

Perhaps its apparent preoccupation with Damian was her mind's way of trying to bring a little respite to the constant pressure she was under, she reasoned half-heartedly, and once again found herself wondering how they might have got on had there not been that in-built wall of hostility between them. She knew the Irish were renowned for their way with words, yet Damian's wit was razor-sharp and cutting and, despite so often finding herself on the receiving end of it, she still found it almost mesmerisingly attractive... just as she did the softly drawled inflexions of his speech. In fact, she found just about every aspect of Damian Sheridan disproportionately fascinating, she informed herself dejectedly, and gained little comfort from reminding herself how sorely in need of mental distraction she was—not only from unrelieved pressure, but from the fact that the actual work she was doing was boring beyond reason!

'Riveting,' drawled Damian, tossing the notes on to the desk and leaning back in the chair he had drawn up beside hers. 'It's a wonder you manage to keep awake, having to sift through all that dross. It's hardly likely to leap into the bestsellers list once it's published, now, is it?'

Rosanne flashed him an uncertain look, his words triggering off something that had been niggling at the back of her mind. Perhaps she should have rung

Lawrence Hastings, her co-owner in Bryant Publishing and its managing director, she thought nervously, and asked for his opinion.

He being one of her grandfather's oldest friends and, she had often suspected, one whom he had confided in totally, it was Lawrence who had overseen her having the training that had made it possible for her to do this job.

But her overall knowledge of publishing was minimal and it was, she suspected, simply her own ignorance causing her to feel as puzzled as she did by her professional dealings with Hester Cranleigh.

'Don't you think it's about time you got around to spitting it out?' demanded Damian sourly, his demeanour indicating, as it so often did, that he was here only reluctantly—an attitude Rosanne found infuriating, given that it was he who had insisted on such meetings.

'To spitting what out?' she asked coldly, her face tightening with the effort it took to control her anger.

'Whatever it is you're so laboriously turning over in your mind,' he replied. 'For one so inclined towards secrecy, you can be extraordinarily transparent at times.'

'I'm not secretive,' she denied hotly, then almost groaned aloud as she realised that during the past couple of weeks her fear of giving herself away must have made her seem almost paranoidly secretive.

'How exactly do you see yourself, darling—as an open book?' he murmured derisively. 'Dinner after dinner, I've listened in awe to your masterly parrying of every single question Hester has put to you. In fact, I'm so nearly convinced you've something to hide that I'm toying with the idea of putting a private detective on you—just for the heck of it,' he finished off casually.

Rosanne struggled to keep a grip on herself as she heard her own sharp intake of breath.

'Feel free,' she retorted with as much careless concern as she could muster. 'Though it seems criminal to waste that sort of money merely to have it confirmed I'm a normal, humdrum sort of girl doing a job she enjoys and who happens to have a perfectly healthy penchant for privacy.'

'Now that was a minefield of a statement, if ever I've heard one,' he stated softly, his narrowed eyes coolly assessing. 'Humdrum your life may be, but normal it most certainly isn't, judging by what little Hester has managed to worm out of you in these past couple of weeks.'

Rosanne gritted her teeth in frustration with herself for having so rashly placed herself at the mercy of his incisive tongue.

'In fact,' he continued relentlessly, 'that primly virginal picture you've managed to paint of yourself has put ideas into her head—if I'm not mistaken, she harbours the delusion we could be turned into an item.'

'Into a what?'

'Into a couple,' he replied, eyeing her coldly. 'Or rather into a billing and cooing couple of lovebirds— Hester's constantly on the look-out for the girl of her dreams for me,' he added morosely.

'Forgive me if this sounds obtuse,' said Rosanne, only just resisting a strong urge to pick up her keyboard and smash it over his head, 'but your terribly subtle approach to me on the day I arrived led me to believe that you had every intention that we should become what you refer to as an item.'

'Yes, but not the sort of item Hester has in mind,' he replied, without so much as a flicker of embarrassment. 'I've a nasty feeling she has Bridie standing sentry outside your bedroom door by night,' he added with an exaggerated sigh.

'Bridie?' echoed Rosanne, having difficulty keeping her face straight.

'She'd hardly entrust something like that to James, now, would she?' he murmured innocently, while his eyes twinkled lasciviously.

'I'm sure she wouldn't,' replied Rosanne. She really had to admire his gall, she thought weakly. He had made it quite plain that, whatever dreams Hester might have on his behalf, she herself didn't feature in his own—yet now he was flirting with her! 'Anyway, I thought Hester had plans for you and the slavishly adoring Nerissa,' she added as an uncharacteristically demure afterthought.

'You really are most unobservant, Ros,' he sighed. 'That threatened dinner invitation to the Blakes hasn't materialised since you arrived on the scene—to my mind a most ominous development.' He suddenly flashed her the most wicked of smiles. 'You know how I live in terror of Hester—not to mention Bridie—and wouldn't, therefore, dare lay so much as a finger on you without extreme provocation.'

'Very wise,' murmured Rosanne, more than a little surprised to find herself responding so easily in kind to this almost indolent flirtation in which he was indulging.

'So how about your sneaking along to my room tonight? I'm in sore need of a dose of slavish adoration.'

Rosanne managed to compose her face into a look of deep contemplation, then shook her head with a sigh of regret.

'It's not that there would be any problem in my getting to your room undetected,' she murmured, straight-faced and earnest. 'It's the slavish adoration I'd fall down on— you see, I've only ever been on the receiving end of that sort of thing.' She gave an apologetic little shrug to round off her words.

'So, you actually do possess a sense of humour,' he murmured with a deep, rumbling chuckle.

'Who says I was being humorous?' queried Rosanne innocently, while a censorious voice from within warned her that, however much in need she might feel of distraction from the pressures she was under, kidding herself that she could get away with a bit of mild flirtation with a man like Damian Sheridan only went to show how dangerously naïve she could be where men were concerned.

His broad shoulders rose then fell in the merest of shrugs. 'You still haven't got around to telling me what was bothering you a few moments ago.'

Caught off guard, Rosanne accepted that she would only flounder unconvincingly if she didn't opt for honesty.

'It's not exactly bothering me,' she began—and realised exasperatedly that she was in danger of floundering anyway. 'It's probably my lack of experience in this job—this is the first time I've done this sort of work on my own... I've always been an assistant to someone experienced until now.'

'So—what's your problem?' he demanded with no trace of sympathy.

'I haven't a problem,' she retorted sharply. 'It's just that Mrs Cranleigh——'

'Hester!' he cut in exasperatedly. 'Everyone calls her Hester and I've lost count of the number of times she's asked you to do likewise.'

'And I try to remember!' exclaimed Rosanne defensively. 'It's just that I'm not used to calling someone of her age by her first name!' Especially not her own grandmother, she reminded herself in silent resentment.

'So—what's Hester's problem?'

'I didn't say she had a problem either,' protested Rosanne. 'It's just that I find her attitude to her husband's biography a little unusual. I mean, I thought she'd be doing the actual writing herself, but she tells me she's not.'

'Cedric Lamont's agreed to do that for her,' stated Damian, very much to her surprise. 'Hester's no writer.'

'So why am I working here with Mrs...with Hester, instead of with Mr Lamont?' she asked in bemusement.

'You're the one who works for Bryant's, not me,' he retorted with a shrug, then added, 'But I do happen to know that Lamont's adored Hester from afar ever since they were kids—and I'm damned sure a biographer of his stature wouldn't have touched the saintly George's life history with a barge-pole if it had been anyone other than Hester asking him to do so. He's obviously made it plain, though, that he's not prepared to do any of the donkey work.'

'Yes, but——' Rosanne broke off with a sigh of frustration, leaning back heavily in her chair. 'Perhaps you're right; her heart isn't really in it.'

'And that's causing you problems, is it?' he queried in tones of biting sarcasm. 'How terribly inconsiderate of the old dear.' There was scorn burning in his eyes as he continued. 'I warned you from the start no good would come from raking up old hurts, so don't be looking for my shoulder to cry on now that Hester's started coming round to my way of thinking.'

'I can't think of any reason for you to say she's coming round to your way of thinking,' snapped Rosanne. 'And, as for raking up old hurts, you know perfectly well that nothing I've covered really touches Mr Cranleigh's private life in any depth——' She broke off, frowning slightly, then added, 'I suppose she'll be arranging with Mr Lamont for the inclusion of the more personal aspects of his life?'

'I've already told you, Lamont's not interested in doing any of the donkey work,' he muttered. 'And besides, what's wrong with this simply being a record of George's public achievements?'

'Because it's meant to be a *biography* of the man,' retorted Rosanne impatiently. 'And a biography——'

'I'm perfectly capable of defining the word for myself, thank you,' he interrupted caustically. 'Though it appears that a sanitised version of his public life is all his faithful is going to get,' he continued, his expression almost smug. 'I say that with some confidence because Hester hasn't handed the personal diaries over to you—and, not having done so by now, I can't see her ever doing so.'

'Are you talking about Hester's own diaries?' asked Rosanne, her uncertainty betrayed in her voice.

He gave a humourless laugh as he shook his head.

'What you've got are little more than the old boy's desk diaries—even his secretaries, you must have noticed, made jottings in them!' he exclaimed derisively. 'But the saintly George was given to "Dear Diary" sessions of a much more private nature. And it's in those that you would find the truth—if ever you got your eager little hands on them.'

'What do you mean—the truth?' demanded Rosanne, her head reeling, though not entirely from the shock of learning there were further diaries, the existence of which Hester had never even hinted at. So much seemed to be hinted at in Damian's sneering words.

'For God's sake, the man was a politician!' he exclaimed dismissively. 'Yet one, according to those records you've been going through, whose career flowed onwards and upwards without so much as a ripple of any form of contention to ruffle its smooth progress.'

'Are you saying he was dishonest in some way?' challenged Rosanne, the barely acknowledged hope that at last she might hear something concrete dying in her as

she realised that this was probably yet another example
of his venting his spleen against the man he so disliked.

'Yes! Use your head, damn it, Ros!' he exclaimed exasperatedly. 'I'm not for one moment suggesting he was
a crook. But can you think of a single prominent politician who hasn't, at one time or another during his
career, been through a sticky patch?'

'No, but——'

'No—precisely,' he snapped. 'It's common knowledge there were members of his own party who would
have happily lynched him over the farm subsidy fiasco.
Then there was——'

'All right, you've made your point,' cut in Rosanne
impatiently. 'But you can't label him dishonest just because he viewed his political career through the same
lavishly tinted spectacles all politicians tend to wear!'
My God, she thought weakly, they were discussing the
man she loathed above all others—and she was virtually
reduced to sticking up for him!

'I obviously made a serious error when I judged you
to possess a brain,' he informed her disgustedly. 'For
God's sake, woman, can't you see that the claptrap politicians come out with is one thing, but that dishing up
that same claptrap in a biography is an entirely different
matter?'

'You may consider it your God-given right to speak
to people in that manner,' exclaimed Rosanne angrily,
leaping to her feet, 'but I have no intention whatever of
listening to any more of it!'

'Sit down!' he roared, on his feet and towering above
her with a speed that startled her. He placed his hands
on her shoulders, their weight forcing her back down on
to the chair. 'How the hell else do you expect to be
spoken to?' he demanded aggressively, leaning back
against the desk-top as he removed his hands and
glowered down at her. 'You should know me well enough

by now to know that I'm not in the least interested in
the ups and downs of George Cranleigh's career...but
I'm darned sure Bryant Publishing is.'

Rosanne's flashed him a murderous look.

'If I were you, darling,' he murmured silkily, 'and I
wanted to hang on to this job for a little longer than six
months, I'd be letting Bryant's know they're wasting their
time—and you can be sure wasting their time is all they're
doing when the subject's widow refuses to give you access
to the necessary material.'

'I'm most touched by your concern for my future em-
ployment,' stated Rosanne from between clenched teeth.
'But it isn't exactly as though Hester's refused me access
to anything yet.'

'You didn't even know of the existence of those diaries
until I mentioned them just now,' he taunted, then
hooked his thumbs into his pocket vents and gazed morosely down at his feet. 'Did you?' he demanded forcefully when she made no reply.

'That's beside the point,' retorted Rosanne, all too
aware how very much to the point it was and thoroughly
unsettled by the fact.

'Look—we can bicker on like this *ad nauseam*!' he
exclaimed bitterly. 'But if you're under the impression
I get some sort of perverted kick out of these interminable daily meetings, you couldn't be more wrong.' He
paused, his eyes rising to flicker lazily over her seated
figure. 'Any kicks I envisage getting from your stay here
are, I can assure you, of an entirely different nature.'

'And that blatantly sexist gibe is supposed to reassure
me in some strange way or another, is it?' snapped
Rosanne, angry colour flooding her cheeks.

'Dear me—was that a sexist gibe?' he enquired with
wide-eyed innocence. 'Being no more than a simple
country lad, I'd never have guessed.'

'I believe you mentioned something about our bickering *ad nauseam*,' she reminded him pointedly.

'You're right—I did,' he muttered, straightening suddenly and walking over to one of the tall windows.

Puzzled, Rosanne twisted round to gaze over to where he now stood with his back to her, his shoulder muscles flexing beneath the tautened material of his shirt as he raised his arms and stretched long and hard. Of all the people she had ever met, she thought frustratedly, Damian Sheridan was the one person she had never been able to gauge with even the slightest measure of success. She had come here fully accepting that she would be constantly on edge in the presence of Hester Cranleigh, but, in comparison with her nerve-racking encounters with this wholly unpredictable man, her meetings with the old lady were almost relaxing!

'The trouble is, Ros, I don't seem to be able to get through to you,' he sighed as he dropped his arms.

Rosanne's eyebrows rose almost to her hairline.

'So what am I supposed to do,' she enquired sarcastically, 'give you a few pointers on how to lure me into your bed?'

He gave a soft laugh as he turned to face her, his huge frame silhouetted darkly against the dying light filtering in through the window.

'Rest assured, darling, that if or when I really start putting my mind to getting you into my bed that's precisely where you'll land.'

'You really do regard yourself as God's gift to women, don't you?' she exclaimed incredulously, her entire body tensing imperceptibly as he began walking back towards her.

'No—I certainly don't consider myself that,' he murmured easily. 'Perhaps it's just a case of my being that bit more adept than the next man at reading the signals you women put out... but that isn't what's on my mind right at this moment.' He squatted before her on his haunches, a brooding darkness in his eyes the only expression discernible in his otherwise impassive face. 'What's on my mind is how to break through that callous shell that seems to encase your heart.'

Rosanne made no attempt to reply, inwardly flinching at the contempt in his tone.

'What is it about you, Ros?' he continued harshly. 'Can it really be that you're so stubborn, so pigheadedly stupid that you'd risk your job rather than admit defeat?'

'For heaven's sake—why all this drama?' she protested, her forced flippancy masking the profoundly disturbing manner in which his contemptuous words were affecting her.

'It was a waste of breath trying to get through to you!' he exclaimed bitterly. 'I tried honesty—admitting how worried I was about how all this raking over of the past would affect Hester. Unfortunately, I wasn't aware that I was attempting to appeal to a better nature that you simply don't possess.'

'It's all so easy for you, isn't it, Damian?' exploded Rosanne recklessly, cut to the quick by those damning words. 'You sit here in your ivory tower, cocooned by privilege, and think you have a God-given right to judge others! It wouldn't even occur to you that the values on which you base those judgements could be worthless! You——' She broke off, stunned into awareness of what was blurting from her as he rose and glowered down at her, his face a cold mask of fury.

'I what?' he demanded icily, his words hoarse with disgust.

Rosanne's eyes dropped from his, the sensation of the colour draining from her face a chilling sharpness on her skin. This was the second time he had provoked her into losing her temper and blurting out far too much.

'My God, you really are a screwed-up little bitch!' he exploded, grasping her by the arms and yanking her roughly to her feet. 'You've a chip on your shoulder the size of a fully grown oak! What the hell do you expect— that I apologise for the wealth I possess and for the fact I haven't led the miserable existence you obviously consider yourself to have led?'

'Damian, I——'

'No! I haven't finished!' he roared over her choked protest. 'You may not understand what it is to love another person as I love that frail old lady upstairs— but you'd better believe I'd destroy anyone who brings her any hurt in these, her last days.' He released her arms with a groan of exasperation. 'Hell, Ros, I know you wouldn't deliberately set out to hurt her!' he exclaimed passionately. 'And it's not simply that you seem incapable of understanding what she's suffered in the past. She's delightful and lovable...yet you freeze her out whenever she tries to open you out. All she's doing is displaying the genuine warmth and affection that's her nature, yet you seem incapable either of accepting it or giving the slightest bit back in return.'

'I loved my grandfather!' blurted out Rosanne, trying to blot out with the sound of her own voice that other crying out within her that, far from not wanting to hurt Hester Cranleigh deliberately, it was something she had been planning for months. 'I loved him every bit as much as you love Hester!' she added vehemently.

'Did you?' he sighed, rubbing his hands wearily against his face. 'Well, perhaps you should try a spot of role reversal. Imagine this was you trying to protect him as I want to protect Hester.'

'Of course I'd have done anything in my power to protect him,' she retorted, her mind filling with the memories of the savage hurts that nothing could have spared either herself or her grandfather. 'But I wouldn't have taken it upon myself to discount his wishes as though they were secondary to what I considered best for him,' she added sharply, those memories steeling her.

'You're implying that my concern is tantamount to insulting Hester's intelligence?'

'If you want to put it like that—yes,' she replied. 'However painful it may be for her, it's Hester's wish that this biography be undertaken.' But was it? she asked herself wearily, her head spinning... There was nothing that she was absolutely sure of any more, except this terrible secret locked in her heart and driving her remorselessly on.

'But she's backing off,' he muttered, shaking his head angrily. 'She hasn't given you the diaries...she didn't even mention them to you!'

'So far—no,' agreed Rosanne. And without them, she suddenly realised, she would learn nothing.

'And if she never does?' he demanded warily.

'If she doesn't, I suppose you're right, there would be little point in my remaining here.'

He said nothing, merely nodded, but relief shone with a startling brilliance in his eyes.

'Damian, could I ask you something?' she said as an uncomfortable thought suddenly occurred to her.

'Fire away,' he replied.

'Have you read those diaries?'

'Good God, no!' he exclaimed, obviously taken aback. 'What makes you ask?'

'Because it's almost as though you're convinced they contain something...well, something unpleasant.'

His eyes narrowed slightly and he gave an unconvincingly dismissive shrug before turning away from her and walking once more over to the window.

'I've already told you I hadn't a lot of time for the man,' he muttered. 'But when I say you'll find the truth in his diaries I'm not suggesting they'll reveal a secret life of crime, if that's what you're thinking.'

Rosanne got to her feet and joined him by the window. She had a strong feeling he was being evasive and was determined to be able to watch his face when he next spoke—just in the faint chance that it might betray him.

'That's not what I thought,' she said, choosing her words carefully as she continued. 'But it seems to me that you're frightened of something more than the memories that would be awakened in Hester by going over them.'

'Well, you're wrong,' he retorted harshly. 'It's solely those memories that bother me...it's too complicated for you to understand.'

'Perhaps you should let me be the judge of that,' she persisted.

He flashed her a scowling look before leaning his head against the window.

'From what I've heard, Hester and George's marriage only just survived their daughter's death...but things were never the same between them.'

Rosanne waited for him to continue, conscious of a private battle being waged within him.

'Having seen them together over all those years, I'd say it was a certainty that they'd never been able to talk out between themselves what had happened...I can't ever remember George mentioning Faith's name in all that time.'

'But you think he wrote about her in his diaries?'

He nodded. 'He had to have some outlet and it's a fair bet his diaries reflect all his deepest feelings at that time. But the thing that worries me most about all this is that I honestly don't believe that Hester has been able to bring herself to read them.'

Rosanne reached over and placed a hand on his arm in a gesture of comfort that was completed before she had any time to realise what she was doing. He was no part of the terrible deeds that had brought her here, she reminded herself despondently. And neither could she blame him for the fact that it was his face that had taken to leaping into her mind with disconcerting frequency and filling her with feelings more suited to an adolescent tempestuously awakening to the opposite sex than an allegedly mature twenty-four-year-old. And whatever his faults—and her disturbing susceptibility to his obvious charms hadn't, mercifully, succeeded in blinding her to a single one of them—she couldn't help but be moved by the protective intensity of his love for Hester Cranleigh.

'Tell me, Ros,' he murmured, glancing down at her hand still resting against his arm, 'is it merely a trick of this poor light—or am I seeing a glimmer of something akin to compassion struggling for expression in your eyes?'

She snatched away her hand, furious with herself for her weakness and with him for his sarcastic rejection of her action.

'You seem to think I'm incapable of understanding how you must feel,' she replied in a stiff, cold voice.

'Perhaps,' he conceded. 'Though I doubt if you're aware of how I'm feeling right at this very moment,' he added, turning and facing her fully.

Rosanne's eyes rose to his. Though there was little in the enigmatic blue of his gaze to warrant such a reaction, she felt the colour flame hotly on her cheeks.

'A blush,' he murmured. 'Now, isn't that a rare and lovely sight?' The instant he had uttered the words he was frowning, as though irritated at having been distracted. 'Anyway, to get back to what we were discussing . . . I'm perfectly aware that I've no right to try to influence Hester one way or another in this matter.'

The unexpectedness of his admission brought an abrupt halt to the orgy of embarrassment in which Rosanne was still wallowing.

'For heaven's sake!' he exclaimed angrily, plainly interpreting her surprise as scepticism. 'I know I have tried to influence her, but it was never a question of my insulting her intelligence by doing so...both she and I know the final decision will be hers and hers alone.'

'But you do feel that, even having taken it as far as having me here, she's decided not to continue?'

He nodded, but his expression lacked conviction.

'With Hester, one can never really be certain—which is why I think it's time I raised the subject of those damned diaries with her...vacillating like this is doing nobody any good.'

'You're probably right,' agreed Rosanne. And it would probably make life a whole lot simpler if Hester Cranleigh were to give up the idea of the biography, she told herself with a sensation of almost light-headed detachment—because then she knew exactly what action she would have to take. 'I'd better put some lights on in here—it's practically dark,' she added briskly.

'Don't you feel safe in the dark with me?' he taunted softly, his fingers reaching out to brush lightly against her cheek. 'Ros?'

Rosanne made a movement of her head that was neither a nod nor a shake. The sensation that his touch had left on her cheek seemed to grow in momentum till it seared through her body and trapped the breath in her lungs.

'Ros?' he repeated teasingly.

This time she managed a positive shake of her head, but her mind had become preoccupied with trying to imagine how her full name would sound spoken in that softly drawling accent of his.

'You don't feel safe with me?'

'No, I don't!' The trapped breath exploded from her in that unguarded admission.

'And there I was, planning to show you around the stables in the morning.' He sighed theatrically. 'Or won't you feel safe with me in daylight either?'

'You said you didn't want women cluttering up your stables when Joe offered to take me round them,' she protested faintly and was more than a little surprised to hear the words, given that her entire system appeared to be running amok on her.

'Did I?' he enquired innocently. 'Well, I dare say I'll be able to show you around far more tidily than Joe ever could. So... will you come?'

She nodded—an action that simply happened of its own accord.

'Good. And if you promise not to frighten my ponies I'll try not to frighten you again.'

It wasn't that he frightened her, thought Rosanne dazedly as he drew her into his arms—he terrified her! She was a person who was used to being in complete control of herself, and not being so was terrifyingly alien to her. Could there really be something so perverse in her nature, she asked herself frantically as his head began lowering to hers, that simply because circumstances rendered him so utterly out of bounds she automatically found him irresistible?

When his mouth began lazily exploring hers, it was the unresisting warmth of her welcome that drew a soft gasp from him before he momentarily lifted his head.

'Now this is a Ros I could so easily acquire a taste for,' he murmured huskily, his body tensing sharply as his lips recaptured hers with unbridled enthusiasm.

Her arms rose to clasp tightly around his neck and a reckless joy seemed to possess her body as her mouth parted in moist acquiescence to the deepening demands of his. There was no part of her able to pay heed to that small voice of desolation crying out from deep within her that this was a man for whom she could well acquire a taste—one that it could well take her a lifetime to assuage.

CHAPTER FOUR

'I'M NOT really in the mood for work today,' sighed Hester Cranleigh, casting a cursory eye over the printouts Rosanne had handed her before tossing them aside on the bed.

Rosanne drew a chair up to the bed and sat down, the thought leaping to her mind that not once, since she had arrived, had there ever been a day when Hester Cranleigh had shown anything even remotely approaching enthusiasm for their task. It was a thought she refrained from putting into words.

'Damian tells me he took you over the stables this morning,' continued the old lady, her eyes twinkling. 'Were you impressed?'

'Oh, yes!' exclaimed Rosanne, her eyes shining. 'I'd absolutely no idea what to expect—but it was fantastic!'

'Damian's always had a way with animals,' murmured Hester. 'And it was a godsend he'd already gone into breeding before he had to give up competitive play——' She broke off with a small shudder. 'I never really did get the hang of the game, and even though I know he was among the top handful of players in the world I lived in constant fear of the boy killing himself on the field... Mind you, he came mighty close to it in that accident.'

'I've never even seen a polo match—though I must say I'd rather like to now,' admitted Rosanne. 'I'd no idea Damian actually broke in the ponies himself.'

The old lady pulled a face. 'And more fool him,' she muttered. 'They're nasty, vicious little brutes for the most part ... And what's that smirk for, young lady?' she demanded, the twinkle back in her eyes.

'Damian told me about how you slander his ponies,' chuckled Rosanne, the invigorating pleasures of her morning sortie having left her more relaxed than she had ever been since her arrival. 'He seems to put it all down to a Shetland pony you once had as a child.'

'And a cantankerous little devil he was too,' snorted Hester. 'Give me a good Irish hunter any day, rather than those nippy little South American things Damian rears.'

'But they all seemed so good-natured,' protested Rosanne laughingly. 'I was terrified of horses until this morning.'

'Horses are easily managed once you know a little about them,' replied the old lady, settling herself comfortably back against a mound of pillows. 'But men are a different matter. Take Damian, for instance. It would be a very foolish girl who didn't watch herself around him now that he's changed his tactics ... and I dare say you've noticed he has charm by the barrowload when he sets his mind to it,' she added archly.

'All he did was show me round his stables,' protested Rosanne, blushing to her roots.

'You're one of the privileged few,' retorted Hester. 'And it also appears he's given up that ridiculous carryon of vetting your work before I see it ... Am I right?'

Rosanne struggled not to show her surprise; she had had no idea that Hester was aware of that arrangement.

'Today's probably just an exception,' she replied. 'He had a meeting with someone and said he probably wouldn't be around to go over things with me.'

The old lady gave a dismissive shrug. 'But he's managed to charm the roses to your cheeks,' she persisted. 'And brought a delightful sparkle to your eyes ... No, don't go shrinking back into that cold little shell of yours,' she chided. 'I much prefer this delightful new Ros.'

Conscious of being thoroughly scrutinised, Rosanne began tensing automatically. She *had* felt like a new person, she realised deflatedly...and all because one man had turned on a bit of charm and shown her over the place. But it wasn't just the mercurial Damian's spell she was in danger of succumbing to; it was also that of this frail old lady to whom she felt almost hypnotically drawn.

'Just for one moment—when you blushed then—it was as though I were seeing my darling Faith beside me again.'

Rosanne's eyes flew in consternation to those of the old women in the bed.

'It's strange how I've never caught the likeness before,' mused Hester, a far-away look in her eyes. 'But then a mind as old as mine is bound to get up to tricks now and then.'

Rosanne's eyes remained locked on the frail figure in the bed, almost willing the anger and bitterness to materialise within her. Then her eyes dropped, dark and uncertain. It was as though the agony of love that had spilled into those words 'my darling Faith' was interfering with her capacity to react normally.

'Faith was my daughter,' said Hester, her words not quite steady. 'She was quite a few years younger than you when she died...and when a part of me died too.'

Rosanne leapt distractedly to her feet, her every instinct crying out to offer comfort—perhaps even forgiveness—to this vulnerable old woman who was her only living grandparent and whose love for her long-lost daughter still lived on so undeniably within her.

Her face deathly pale, she slumped back down on to her seat, a last remaining thread of steel still holding her back.

'Ros, I've obviously upset you!' exclaimed Hester contritely. 'I'm so sorry, my dear. It's just that I seem to have been dwelling in the past so much of late.'

'That's only to be expected,' managed Rosanne, her voice peculiarly strained. 'I mean . . . getting all this material together, it's bound to bring up sad memories.'

'You mean George's wretched biography?' snorted Hester, swiftly returning to her old self. 'There's no need to be diplomatic, my dear. I'd have thought it was pretty obvious that's the last thing that's been occupying my mind!' Her response to Rosanne's struggle for a noncommittal expression was a loud sigh. 'I suppose I haven't really been fair on you—but the diaries should make up for that. I've decided to give them to you . . . George's *real* diaries.'

Rosanne couldn't be sure what sort of expression would have found its way to her face had she not been exercising superhuman control over herself as those words sank in, but her voice, when she at last managed to speak, was barely recognisable.

'Does that mean you've decided to take an interest in the biography now?' she croaked, thrown to find how strangely ambivalent her reaction to this bombshell was.

'No! That's not what I mean at all,' replied Hester, her tone uncharacteristically sharp. 'I——' She broke off as the door of the room opened. 'So—you've decided to come to spy on what's been passed on to me after all, have you, Damian?' she called out accusingly.

Rosanne turned to find Damian striding across the room, his tall, dynamic presence sending her pulses leaping with a swift violence that she fought to subdue with equal violence.

He leaned over the bed and kissed Hester's cheek.

'Go away—you stink of horses!' she complained irritably.

'Your favourite smell, darling,' he retorted, grinning over at Rosanne as he sat himself down on the bed. 'So—what's put you in this angelic mood?' he teased. 'Ros been giving you a hard time, has she?'

Hester reached up and gave his cheek a perfunctory pat.

'You need a shave!' he mimicked in a falsetto imitation of her voice.

'And so you do!' retorted Hester grumpily, but the undeniable bond of love between them, despite that tone, brought a churning sensation to Rosanne's stomach.

And there was so much love between them, she thought almost enviously, before hastily reminding herself that she and her grandfather had been blessed with a love just as deep. Yet as her eyes alighted on the dark, vibrantly glossy head inclining towards the snowy white of Hester Cranleigh's she was hearing words her grandfather had once spoken to her, whispering teasingly in her ears.

'You ought to be getting out and meeting some eligible young men. What are you waiting for—your prince to materialise out of thin air? Though that's what he'll have to be, the man who wins my Rosanne's heart—a prince among men.'

Then it was the soft Irish music of Damian's voice blurring in her ears and she was remembering her first sight of him and the thoughts of Celtic princes that had leapt to her mind.

'Heaven preserve us, what have I walked in on?' demanded Damian, exasperation stripping the music from his tones. 'There's Hester greeting me like a leper and Ros skulking in her chair in silence!'

'I'm not skulking!' protested Rosanne.

'Of course she isn't,' confirmed Hester. 'I've never seen her in a sunnier mood.'

'Am I to take it I'm the cloud that's suddenly blocked out all the sunshine?' he chuckled, cocking his head and giving Rosanne a playful look of melancholy that threatened to melt her bones.

'He's so sensitive—aren't you, darling?' murmured Hester, her eyes once more twinkling as she reached up and ruffled his hair.

'OK,' he grinned, shrugging. 'I'll mind my own business.'

Hester gazed up at him, guardedness entering her expression. 'We were talking about Faith,' she told him quietly.

The atmosphere in the room altered perceptibly, but exactly how, Rosanne was unable to gauge—just as she was similarly unable to gauge what it was that flickered momentarily over Damian's face. But she found herself inordinately moved at the sight of his strong, darkly tanned hand reaching over and enveloping one of Hester's in its hugeness.

'The time had to come,' murmured Hester gently.

'Yes,' agreed Damian, though plainly not at ease. 'Hessie, you do understand, don't you, why I've been so against this damned biography?' he blurted out.

'Hessie,' chuckled the old lady. 'You haven't called me that in years... Of course I understand.' She shook her head sadly. 'But the fact that I've rarely been able to bring myself to speak of my daughter over the years— even to you, my darling boy, whom I love as much as if you'd been her baby brother—doesn't mean that my memories of her have ever faded.'

'I know that,' he protested almost angrily. 'But I also know that you'd never have got yourself involved in anything like this wretched biography if George hadn't demanded it of you!'

'Damian, he didn't *demand* it.'

'Perhaps not in so many words!' he exclaimed bitterly. 'But the fact that he wanted it has been niggling away at the back of your mind ever since he died. Your heart's never been in it—and it isn't now, no matter what you say!'

'The trouble with you, my darling boy, is that there are times when you refuse to accept that things might not be as you choose to see them,' sighed Hester. 'But no matter—Ros has helped me to see that I've no option but to give her George's real diaries.'

'Has she, now?' muttered Damian, a baleful coldness in his eyes as they flickered dismissively in Rosanne's direction. 'So that, as they say, is that.'

'Yes, it is,' replied Hester firmly. 'And now that we've dispensed with that subject, we'll turn to another. It's about time you started showing Ros around a bit more—her trip to the stables this morning did her the world of good. Why don't you take her to a match? She tells me she's never been to one.'

Almost paralysed with embarrassment, Rosanne couldn't bring herself to look at either of them.

'Oh, yes?' drawled Damian, rolling from the bed to his feet in one fluid movement. 'And while we're off gadding around the countryside who, may I ask, will be running this place?'

'Darling, don't tell me you're going to turn out a bad loser,' sighed Hester, her expression perplexed as she gazed up into his scowling face.

'That's hardly the issue,' he murmured, his expression softening noticeably. 'Since when has anyone ever been able to talk you out of something you'd set your mind on?'

The old lady chuckled, then lay back against the pillows. 'Now off you go, the pair of you; I can feel one of those interminable naps coming on... and I shan't be down for dinner this evening.'

'Are you not feeling too good?' exclaimed Damian, bending anxiously over her.

'Not too good—but nothing a bit of peace and quiet won't put right.'

Her eyes were already closing as Damian bent and kissed her cheek.

Rosanne got to her feet and replaced her chair. Her mind was churning, crammed to overflowing with far too many differing emotions for her to be capable of dealing with a single one of them. There was Hester— no! she objected violently; there was her *grandmother*. Her grandmother for whom she was having difficulty suppressing feelings almost of affection rather than the hatred she deserved. And then there was Damian—who had never even featured in her sketchy mental preparations for her ordeal here; Damian, who had shed his mask of coldness and let the laughter dance in his eyes as he had drawn her even further under his Celtic spell that morning.

But there was nothing even remotely resembling laughter in the eyes impaling hers with their coldness as he closed the door of Hester's room behind them. And there was anger in the pressure of the fingers grasping her arm as he marched her down the hallway towards the stairs.

'Damian, would you mind letting go of my arm?' she asked in as even a tone as she could muster. Something had obviously upset him, she reasoned nervously with herself, but his behaviour could hardly be described as normal and she had no intention of antagonising him further if she could possibly help it.

'I want to talk to you,' he snapped, striding down the stairs with her firmly in tow.

'I can see no reason why you should feel obliged to apply a manual tourniquet to my arm simply because you wish to speak to me,' she retorted, anger seeping into her words as she immediately had second thoughts about pandering to his volatile temperament.

'No, you wouldn't,' he snapped, yanking her so forcefully after him that she promptly lost her footing.

'God save us, is there a fire?' demanded Bridie, appearing in the hallway just as the two of them reached the bottom of the stairs.

'A question I was asking myself, Bridie,' exploded Rosanne as she attempted the almost impossible task of freeing her arm while remaining on her feet without Damian's support.

'Damian, that's no way for a gentleman to behave,' scolded the housekeeper, though there was open amusement on her plump features.

'Bridie, just mind your own business, will you?' growled Damian, then promptly emitted a roar of outrage, releasing Rosanne's arm as she elbowed him in the stomach with her other.

Bridie's reaction was a chortle of delight. 'I warned you the day would come when you'd come up against a woman who'd not let you take the liberties you've come to see as your God-given right,' she pronounced smugly.

'Bridie!' growled Damian warningly, then lunged for Rosanne. 'We'll be in the library—talking,' he said, capturing Rosanne's left hand in his own, then manacling her upper arm with his right for good measure. 'And we don't want an audience!'

'Perhaps you'll be wanting tea?' suggested the housekeeper, unabashedly relishing this unexpected scene and showing not the least sign of being intimidated by her employer's roars.

'No, we shan't!' he exclaimed exasperatedly, then added, 'And, before I forget, Hester won't be down for dinner.'

Bridie's intrigued expression switched instantly to one of shocked concern. 'And there I was, thinking she was in such good form today,' she muttered sadly. 'I'll just go up and peek in on her,' she added, bustling past them and up the stairs, the entertaining spectacle she had been so enjoying gone from her mind.

'And Bridie's not the only one who thought Hester was in such good form,' stated Damian grimly as he marched them off towards the library. 'In fact, she was in such good spirits when I saw her after lunch that I couldn't bring myself to say anything that might spoil it for her,' he continued, flinging open the huge library door, then hurling it shut behind them. 'But no such consideration would even occur to you, would it?' he finished disgustedly, releasing Rosanne just as she was gathering together all her strength to drag herself free.

'My God, you're prehistoric!' she flung at him in fury. 'You may think you can get away with this sort of behaviour with other people, but you're certainly not going to with me!'

'And what sort of behaviour is that, darling?' he enquired, his stance menacing as he scowled down at her.

'You may try to joke about it, but you really do see yourself as some sort of feudal lord——' She broke off to take a breath and to berate herself for ever having considered this overbearing bully in the least attractive. 'You think all you have to do is fling a few crumbs of charm in the direction of us peasants and we'll joyfully submit to being your whipping-boys whenever things don't go quite as you wish!'

'My, but you have a way with words,' he drawled, sitting down on the substantial arm of a huge leather armchair and gazing up at her with an expression of exaggerated concentration. 'I'm afraid you'll have to give me a few moments to unravel that lot. Tell me, is this a tried tactic of yours—resorting to gibberish whenever you're cornered?'

Rosanne opened her mouth to vent her fury, then promptly closed it. What in God's name had she got herself into? she asked herself numbly. What had possessed her even to come here, let alone assume she'd be able to handle it and walk away virtually unscathed?

She tore her eyes away from the handsome face looking up into her own with open mockery, feelings of panic assailing her as she tried to fix her gaze on the book-lined walls of the graceful, high-ceilinged room, only to find her vision blurring drunkenly.

'OK, so what is it that's gone against my wishes that necessitates my using you as a whipping-boy?' he drawled, then added facetiously, 'I do apologise if your original eloquence has been blunted by my inadequate paraphrasing.'

'Just go away and leave me alone!' choked Rosanne, turning her back on him and willing the tears gathering ominously in her eyes not to fall. She *never* cried, she told herself frantically; there had been times when she had craved the release of tears, but they had so rarely ever come... and now this!

'Admit it, Ros, you'd collapse with the shock of it if I did,' he laughed grimly. 'We feudal lords dish out the orders—we never take them.'

'I wasn't issuing an order,' she protested raggedly, the confidence draining from her as she wondered just what it was that was happening to her and for how long she could carry on without making a complete fool of herself. 'Damian, I'm not used to all this ranting and raving for no apparent reason. I'm used to people who, when they feel they have a problem, sit down and discuss it rationally. I simply——'

'My God, you've a nerve, demanding rationality from me!' he bellowed. 'What sort of a creature are you, for heaven's sake? Can you think of no one but yourself? I told you I'd ask Hester about letting you have the diaries, but that wasn't good enough for you, was it?' His face a mask of fury, he took her by the shoulders and shook her angrily. 'No, you had to twist her arm up her back to make sure you got them—and to hell with any consideration of whether or not that was what she really wanted!'

'Damian,' she protested hoarsely as understanding began filtering through to her bemused mind, 'you're completely wrong!'

'Oh—I'm wrong, am I?' he snarled. 'You actually stopped short on the arm-twisting, did you?'

'Damian, it was Hester who brought up the subject of the diaries!'

'And you browbeat her into giving you them!'

'Of course I didn't!' she exclaimed distractedly, oblivious of the tears now streaming down her face. 'She told me she'd made up her mind to let me work from them.'

'You're lying! She said you'd made her see she had no option but to give you them. And you can switch off the waterworks; I'm immune to tricks like that.' His eyes flashing disgust, he released his painful grasp on her shoulders, almost pushing her from him as he did so.

'I can assure you, no one has ever reduced me to tears of rage before,' she informed him frigidly, hating him. 'But then, I've never come across anyone as capable of twisting facts as you are! I don't care how you choose to interpret what Hester said—nothing can alter the fact that it was she who brought up the subject of the diaries, and did so by telling me she was giving me them!'

'I can easily check that with her,' he muttered, but his uncertainty was evident in his tone.

'You can check it as much as you like,' retorted Rosanne icily, 'but the facts will remain the same.'

'Why was she so upset, then?' he demanded, dragging his fingers through the dark thickness of his hair in a gesture of thorough uneasiness.

'Damian, she explained why,' sighed Rosanne, feeling suddenly utterly drained. 'It was talking about . . . about her daughter.'

'Ros, what can I say?' he asked hoarsely. 'Except that I'm sorry and that you've every right to regard me as a raving lunatic.'

'I have to admit the thought crossed my mind,' she conceded wryly, trying to steel herself against the pervasive softness melting through her by reminding herself of just how appallingly he had behaved. 'Heaven knows what poor Bridie must have thought,' she added stiltedly, her mind now inexplicably occupied with wondering what it would be like to be loved—loved to the exclusion of all others—by this man.

'Whatever it was, she'll no doubt embroider it to her own fanciful satisfaction,' he joked with uncharacteristic self-consciousness, his mind plainly not on his words. 'Ros, I——' He broke off, then sat once more on the arm of the chair, his broad shoulders hunching tensely as he gazed down at his feet. 'Hell, I don't really know what to say to you!' he exclaimed exasperatedly.

'Damian, there's nothing more to be said,' she told him quietly. 'You made a mistake and you've apologised. Despite what you may think of me, I can appreciate how much you love Hester and how desperately worried you must be about her well-being.' She appreciated it all right, she told herself with a jittery pang—and it frightened the wits out of her.

'Despite what I think of you?' he queried, his eyes rising in challenge. 'And what exactly is it that I think of you, Ros?'

'For a start you think me capable of browbeating a sick old lady,' she retorted angrily, stunned by his sudden

switch back to aggression ... perhaps she had only imagined his momentary contrition! 'And why should I,
for heaven's sake? You'd already said you'd bring up
the subject of the diaries with her——' She broke off,
deciding she had had enough, and made for the door.

'Where are you going?'

'Anywhere I don't have to listen to you and your manic
ravings!' she exploded, grasping hold of the huge door-
handle. 'I've had enough!'

'Well, I haven't!'

Rosanne let out a squeak of fright as his hand reached
from behind her and firmly removed hers from the door-
handle.

'Don't creep up on me like that!' she shrieked, barely
in control of herself.

'For heaven's sake, come and sit down and pull
yourself together!' he exclaimed, placing a none too light
arm across her shoulders and guiding her back towards
a huge leather chesterfield. 'Ros, it wasn't as facetious
as it might have sounded—my asking you what you consider I think of you.'

'Wasn't it?' she demanded sarcastically. 'And stop
pushing me like that!' she protested furiously as he gave
her a gentle shove that sent her sprawling on to the sofa.

'Sorry,' he muttered, no hint of apology in his tone
as he sat down beside her. 'Ros, I asked you that question
because, quite frankly, I have difficulty making up my
mind what I think of you from one minute to the next.'

Uncertain what to make of that statement, Rosanne
glanced up at him and immediately began scrabbling to
move further from him—he was practically on her knee!

She flung him a withering look as he immediately
moved into the space she had created between them.
'That's hardly my problem,' she informed him frigidly,
removing her arm from where it had become wedged
uncomfortably against the arm-rest.

'Oh, no?' he responded, his eyes glittering icicles. 'I'd say it was very much your problem, darling.'

The Irish, Rosanne had quickly learned, used the word 'darling' as readily as they smiled—Damian included. But there were times, such as now, when Damian managed to wield that endearment with the finesse of a cudgel.

'You see, there's something about you that bothers me, Miss Rosamund Grant...the fact that you seem to have something to hide.'

Rosanne felt as though her skin had become a fragile shell, barely able to contain the fear liquefying within her.

'And what really bothers me, right now, is the fact that you're just sitting there saying nothing.'

'What am I supposed to say?' responded Rosanne tonelessly. What in God's name could she say? 'I came here to do a job, not to——'

'And one you've handled abysmally,' he cut in accusingly. 'You're the one supposed to be drawing out Hester, not the other way round! Yet you clam up and act as though you're being grilled when she asks you a few simple questions about yourself.'

'It's *not* my job to draw out Hester,' she flustered. 'I'm not a writer, I'm here to——'

'You're not damned well here to upset her the way you do with your abandoned-orphan routine!'

'You accuse me of clamming up when she asks me questions and now you say I've upset her with things I've said! Make up your mind, for heaven's sake!'

'You know perfectly well what I mean!' he exclaimed with a groan of pure frustration. 'Hell, it wouldn't surprise me to learn that Hester decided to give you those damned diaries simply because she feels sorry for you!'

'You're the one who brought up the subject of the diaries in the first place!' she rounded on him in angry accusation. 'You were the one who offered to speak to her about giving them to me!'

He grasped her chin in his hand, forcing her face round to his.

'Only because I felt, for Hester's sake, that the issue needed broaching—you didn't figure in my considerations at all,' he informed her candidly. 'And you know it.'

Refusing to meet his gaze, she trained her eyes on the dark green of the leather upholstery behind his head.

'If you feel I'm such a . . . a ghastly person, why would you even consider suggesting she entrust to me something that means so much to her?' she asked stiltedly.

'I didn't say I feel you're a ghastly person,' he muttered, his hand sliding from her chin to her shoulder as he suddenly leaned back. 'Ros, can't you try to see this from my point of view?' he sighed. 'I know I'm overprotective of Hester to the point of paranoia, but she's all the world to me and I've told you, God knows how many times, how I feel about this damned biography. As far as I'm concerned, you're just an added worry in all this.'

For an instant her every instinct was to tell him there was no need for him to worry, but guilt reared up in her and suppressed what would only have been a blatant lie.

'Ros, from the moment you arrived here it's as though you've been constantly on your guard. After a while I began wondering if I'd perhaps hit a vulnerable spot in you by coming on as strong as I did.'

Rosanne now trained her eyes on the book-lined wall at the other end of the room, her blank expression betraying nothing of the army of disquieting emotions marching ruthlessly through her mind.

'Hell, if I find a woman attractive, I react accordingly—it's simply my nature! But now and then I actually made an effort to stifle my normal instincts with you, even though the message I got from you when I took you in my arms——'

'I thought this was supposed to have some bearing on your over-protective attitude towards Hester,' cut in Rosanne sharply, her cheeks flaming.

He let out an angry exclamation and straightened, forcing her to face him once more, this time by grasping her painfully by the shoulders and swinging her round.

'And so it has!' he rasped, hostility burning in his gaze. 'As I say, I thought it was me making you so jittery. But this morning was the nearest I've seen you to a flesh and blood human being over a protracted period, and I got to thinking that perhaps it wasn't me. Then I walked in on you and Hester—hell, I could have cut the air with a knife!'

'I've already explained the atmosphere you walked in on!' she protested wildly, her eyes looking anywhere but at his. 'Why can't you just accept the fact that I'm not used to people like you and Hester...instead of making me feel like some sort of freak!'

'I'm sorry if that's the way I've made you feel,' he muttered gruffly, 'but it's just that I can shake off this feeling that, one of these days, whatever it is you've got simmering inside you is going to blow.' He drew her forward till her cheek rested against his. 'You can blow all the fuses you like around me, but you leave Hester out of whatever it is making you the way you are.'

'I've no intention of blowing a fuse, as you put it, around anyone,' she said, but there was a tremor of uncertainty in her voice, and the warm, vibrant scent of his skin in her nostrils.

He drew his face from hers slightly. 'Perhaps I am being paranoid,' he whispered, sliding his hands slowly down her back and taking her into his arms. 'Perhaps I have got most of it wrong. But don't tell me it's my imagination that the only time I've had a glimpse of the real Ros is when I've got you like this in my arms.'

His mouth crushed down on hers. Though his words had been gentle, there was an angry impatience in the lips parting hers with a bruising force. And as she wound her arms tightly around his neck and her body melted towards his she tried telling herself that she had no choice but to participate in anything that would distract him from further voicing his disturbingly intuitive fears.

'Oh, Ros,' he groaned, his mouth hot and searching against hers as he manoeuvred their bodies till they lay full length on the huge sofa, entwined in one another's arms. 'Why hadn't you the sense to follow your instincts and say "To hell" that first time I kissed you, and for once let the consequences be gloriously damned?' he whispered huskily, his hands deftly assured as he placed them beneath her sweater.

The careless confidence of those hands and the practised ease with which he had manoeuvred their bodies into their present intoxicating closeness sent a niggle of doubt wafting through her mind. Then there was nothing in her mind but the electrifying sensation of the touch of his hands against her flesh as they slid beneath her bra and cupped her breasts. The cry that burst from her was one of startled pleasure and there was laughter in his eyes as he gazed down at her.

'Why try to pretend you're an ice maiden when you know you were made for loving?' he teased softly, his hands playing all the while against her throbbing flesh.

Then the laughter was gone from his eyes and what she saw in its place galvanised her body into resistance of the dark intensity reaching out to engulf her. Yet it was as she moved to extricate her body from the intoxicating nearness of his that she felt the sudden surge of desire leap within him and a soft cry exploded on her lips as she felt that same desire spread its rampaging way throughout her.

'Damian, no...please!' she choked as he pushed aside her sweater and lowered his head to her exposed breasts.

'No—or please?' he whispered, his breath a maddening heat against her flesh.

She tried tensing herself against what was happening to her, but when his lips closed over one almost painfully engorged nipple she gave up, twining her fingers distractedly into his hair while she gave her body up to sharp shocks of excitement bombarding its every nerve-end. When his tongue began creating even more intense havoc than his lips had, there was protest in the groaned cry escaping her and her fingers were tugging wildly in his hair.

'Ouch!' he protested, lifting his head to gaze down at her, the glittering darkness of the desire in his eyes softened by the lazy grin playing on his lips. 'We've wasted far too much time,' he whispered huskily. 'Don't let's waste any more.'

As though in slow motion she saw his head begin lowering once more to hers and already her mouth was quivering in anticipation of the intoxicating delights of his. There was a part of her that cried out for her to say 'To hell' and follow the never-before-awakened needs now clamouring to be met within her body. But there was that core within her that refused to let go and that drove her to turn her head in that moment when his mouth would have repossessed hers.

'No!' Her denial was almost a plea as she pushed him from her and violently tugged down her sweater to cover her nakedness. 'I...I came here to do a job,' she protested distractedly, 'not to provide you with sexual entertainment!'

She knew almost as she was uttering the words that she was lashing out unfairly at him to hide her own shock and confusion. But she couldn't bring herself to retract them; instead she kept her eyes lowered from his, hugging her arms protectively around her torso and hurriedly returning her feet to the safety of the parquet floor when she sensed him move away from her.

'The implication being that I'd have been the only one being entertained—is that it?' he eventually enquired, his voice sounding so utterly impersonal, compared to its seductive softness of only seconds before, that it left Rosanne feeling as though a cold hose had been turned on her.

'Damian, I shouldn't have made that remark... but I'm sorry, I had no right to lead you on like that,' she apologised stiltedly.

'No need to apologise, darling,' he drawled, stretching his long legs out before him as he leaned back against the sofa. 'Nobody's ever been able to lead me anywhere I didn't want to go. But you really shouldn't have stopped, you know,' he added almost conversationally. 'Sex is one of the best relaxants there is—and you're about as uptight as I've ever seen anyone.'

Rosanne felt the sharp sting of her own fingernails digging into her flesh. Seconds ago she had wanted this man as she had never wanted anything in her life before. She had been virtually out of control—a state she certainly never had been in her life before. But she had denied herself and him, and had been able to do so only because she was responding to the most powerful instinct of all—that of survival. In holding back her body, she had been holding back her love... and she was hovering on the brink of loving a man who rated the act of love as no more meaningful than an interlude of relaxing entertainment.

'Personally, I find hot chocolate less of a bother,' she retorted, a terrible hurt spilling venom into her words.

'Perhaps you do, but it doesn't seem to have had the desired effect—or is it simply that you'd be in an even worse state without your daily dose of hot chocolate?'

Rosanne leapt to her feet, her cheeks scarlet with humiliation.

'Perhaps the fact that you breed animals accounts for your farmyard approach to sex,' she flung at him in disgust, then marched off towards the door.

'Stop!' he roared.

She froze in her tracks.

'My, but you're well trained,' he murmured mockingly, from right behind her. 'It's a pity you don't always respond like that. And it's an even greater pity that you could even come out with a remark like that. Now—if you'd said something along the lines of, "Damian, I love another and, despite the fact that I fancy you like hell, I intend remaining true to him,"' he mimicked in an exaggerated parody of her accent, 'or even, "Damian, I've a bit of a problem with sex as I've just had my heart broken"—or whatever—you'd have found me the most understanding of men. But your reference to my farmyard approach to sex—now that, darling, was hypocrisy at its most sublime.'

With that, he strode on past her and out of the room.

Rosanne expelled the breath she hadn't even been conscious of holding as the door closed behind him.

'Well, so much for my prince, Grandpa Ted,' she whispered aloud. 'The role of his princess isn't quite what he has in mind for me.'

But as she too made her way towards the door there was an ache like a lead weight in her heart that stripped the joking lightness from those words and left them echoing forlornly in her ears.

CHAPTER FIVE

'HESTER wants to see you,' announced Damian, striding into the study and scattering its tranquillity with his turbulent presence. 'She's in the blue drawing-room.'

Accepting that the moment she had been dreading all day had arrived, Rosanne turned from her word processor.

'She's up?' she asked.

He was dressed in his usual working clothes: dark sweater, pale riding breeches and deep tan leather boots—and this time, when her heart lurched in sickening, churning excitement at the sight of him, her reaction was no more than a wearily fatalistic mental shrug.

'No—we've just moved the entire contents of the drawing-room upstairs,' he mocked, his eyes totally impersonal as they met hers. 'Of course she's up!'

'I haven't quite finished what I'm doing,' she told him, her tone as impersonal as his eyes, 'but I wanted to talk to you anyway, before I saw Hester.'

'Well, it'll have to wait, she's——'

'It can't wait,' interrupted Rosanne, determined to have her say. 'I've been thinking about what you said yesterday—and you're right.'

He gave her an exaggeratedly questioning look before drawing up a chair and straddling it.

'I said quite a few things yesterday,' he murmured, his tone causing her cheeks to colour instantly. 'Which one in particular are you admitting to my being right about?'

Closing her mind to his goading sarcasm, Rosanne took a steadying breath.

'You're right in that I've never felt able to relax fully in Hester's presence,' she told him quietly. 'At first it was simply because this was my first time doing this sort of work without the back-up of someone more experienced—and I was nervous.'

'And then?' he demanded, his jaw tightening impatiently.

'Then—I suppose it was your saying how harrowing she might find reliving certain memories that affected me,' she pressed on, praying that her confidence, so rapidly draining from her, wouldn't desert her completely. 'I became apprehensive about how she might react.'

'Spit it out, Ros!' he exclaimed impatiently when her words threatened to dry up on her. 'We haven't all day.'

'So, I've decided to contact Bryant's and suggest they send someone more experienced to take over.'

'That should boost your career prospects no end,' he drawled unfeelingly.

'That's my business,' she snapped, but she felt relief racing through her like an invigorating breeze as she reached over and switched off her word processor.

'I suppose your lying awake most of the night as you reached that momentous decision accounts for the sooty rings around your eyes and your generally unappetising appearance today?' he observed unkindly.

Rosanne jammed the cover over the machine, clamping her lips tightly against any reckless retort. She had lain awake for almost the entire night, she reminded herself bitterly, but her decision to leave here at the earliest opportunity had been reached in a relatively short portion of those sluggishly crawling hours.

'And what a shame that you should have spent a sleepless night in vain!' he exclaimed in parodied tones of concern as he returned to his feet. 'Because Hester's decided to do a runner once she's handed over the diaries. She's off to Dublin and, though you'll never get her to admit it, we'll not be seeing her back here until you've got the diaries neatly sorted and out of the way.'

Rosanne gave silent thanks that she was firmly seated, but she still took the precaution of placing her hands on the desk and gripping it tightly for back-up support as she digested this mind-boggling piece of news.

'But I've made up my mind,' she began weakly, her scattered thoughts refusing to be collected.

'You'd made up your mind because of a particular problem you claim to have,' he drawled, sauntering over to the door. 'That problem has just been removed. Now, do you mind getting a move on?'

Rosanne got to her feet, her mind still in complete turmoil.

'Or perhaps you see this as one problem being removed and an even worse one taking its place,' he taunted. 'Are you worried about not being able to trust yourself here alone with me, Ros?'

Rosanne pushed her chair under the desk, squaring her shoulders imperceptibly as she turned towards him.

'I'm worried frantic, darling,' she replied in her best imitation of his drawling tones, 'you being God's most precious gift to womankind and all that.' She flashed him a brittle smile as she walked straight past him and through the doorway. 'But I shall, after all, have the diaries to divert me—let's just pray they'll do the trick.'

And she *would* have the diaries, she thought with a violent start—stunned that this fact should only now be occurring to her. Today she would hold in her hands what could well be the key to all those mysteries that had tormented her over so many years...yet now she seemed incapable of any reaction.

Her steps quickened as she sensed Damian catching up with her. The full impact of it all would probably hit her with a vengeance once she actually had the diaries in her possession, she told herself with grim apprehension.

'God's most precious gift to womankind,' he chuckled from behind her—in fact, from so close behind her that she could almost feel the warmth of his body.

Irritated, Rosanne stopped and he promptly walked straight into her.

'Damian, just stop it, will you?' she exclaimed exasperatedly.

'Now, is that really any way to be addressing God's most precious gift to womankind?' he enquired, leaning his body quite blatantly against hers as he spoke the words against her hair.

'Damian, I'm sure you must find this all terribly amusing,' she snapped, 'whereas I simply find it rather childish.'

Except that it was her deliberately causing him to walk into her that had been childish, she reminded herself accusingly, and the price she was paying was this disturbingly familiar languid softness now melting through her body.

But there was nothing in the least languid in her body's response when he suddenly placed his hands on her hips, his fingers spreading in careless seduction as they curved to accommodate her contours.

'Childish isn't a word I can ever recall any woman using to describe me,' he whispered, lowering his head so that his words sighed against her ear.

Rosanne was conscious of her own stifled gasp as his hands drew her body fully back against his, and wondered if he too had experienced the sudden fire scorching between them.

'I have to admit I've been called——'

'Damian, for heaven's sake!' she exploded, unnerved by the violence of her response and tearing herself from the casual lightness of his hold as though struggling to escape heavy chains. 'I thought we were supposed to be in some sort of a mad rush to see Hester,' she called breathlessly over her shoulder as she sped on ahead of him.

'I can't think what gave you that impression,' he laughed, his easy strides bringing him to the drawing-room door at the same time she reached it. 'After you, darling,' he murmured mockingly, throwing open the door for her.

Hester Cranleigh was seated before a blazing log fire, her slight figure seeming almost lost in the huge, fan-backed chair.

'I hope I didn't drag you from anything important?' she apologised to Rosanne, her features looking drawn and fatigued.

'No, of course you didn't!' exclaimed Rosanne, her guard so lowered by her own tiredness that a sharp pang of anxiety at the old lady's air of complete exhaustion slipped through her defences.

Hester gave a wry smile before returning her gaze to the blazing fire. 'True, I suppose, in that there's little of importance in that study for you to be dragged from,' she murmured, then glanced down at the brown leather attaché case to the side of her chair. 'All the interesting things, I think you'll find, are in there.'

As Damian strode between them and propped himself against the marbled mantelpiece, Rosanne looked across at the case, willing herself to feel something—anything!

'Are you really sure you're up to this trip to Dublin?' she heard herself blurt out, startling Damian, who flashed her an openly surprised look, as much as she had herself. 'It's quite a journey and you look very tired,' she added diffidently.

'Ah, but Hester does these things in style,' murmured Damian, puzzlement still in his eyes. 'Charlie Deeny—a neighbour who's her devoted slave—flies her down in his executive jet, no less.'

'And it beats your lunatic driving any day,' chuckled the old lady, flashing Rosanne one of her wickedly conspiratorial looks. 'I'm sure that, if ever you were in a real hurry to get to Dublin, Damian could no doubt get you there faster by car than Charlie could in his plane... but there are few with the nerves to stomach this rascal's driving.'

'You exaggerate, darling,' muttered Damian.

Rosanne glanced over at the man by the fireplace, puzzled by something in his tone she couldn't quite put her finger on.

'Do I, now?' murmured Hester drily, then frowned. 'Damian, get yourself a chair,' she scolded, 'before you catch fire!'

He shrugged, then pulled a footstool to the side of her chair and sat down on it, looking not in the least comfortable.

'So?' he growled, his tone disgruntled.

Hester gave a loud sigh, then rolled her eyes in exasperation. 'Darling, I don't want you being difficult.'

'I'm not being difficult,' he replied morosely. 'But... hell, what's the use?' he exploded angrily. 'How can you possibly go traipsing off to Dublin?'

'I wondered when you'd get around to getting that off your chest,' she sighed, motioning him nearer.

When he obediently leaned over towards her, she began gently stroking his hair.

As she had so often, Rosanne found herself watching, almost in envy, the unselfconscious affection that they so openly displayed. But the grimness of anxiety on Damian's face tugged fiercely at her heartstrings and she wondered at her own stupidity in not realising how strongly opposed to this trip he was bound to be—no matter how he had tried to hide the fact.

'Dr Moore's quite happy about it,' continued Hester. 'In fact, he's arranging for me to go into the Dublin clinic for a couple of days while I'm down there—to have those tests he's been on about.'

'But that's not the reason you're going,' muttered Damian, unappeased.

'Of course it's not,' chuckled Hester, then added briskly, 'but we both know I haven't much time left and that I can't go without saying goodbye to my darling Dublin—now can I?'

Rosanne felt herself shiver involuntarily on hearing those so casually honest words, but those that followed sent a peculiar tingling sensation coursing down her spine.

'And you know that not a single week's gone by since they were last up here that Rosanne and Hank haven't been pestering me to go down and stay with them.'

Rosanne! Her mother's dearest friend and the woman after whom she herself had been named.

'And yes, darling,' sighed Hester, when Damian made no response, 'I suppose you could say I'm still running from the same thing I've been running from for over twenty years now.'

Damian sat bolt upright. 'And that's nobody's business but yours,' he protested passionately. 'It's just that I hate the thought of your being driven from here just because of that damned biography!'

'Darling, I think it's about time I made things a little clearer.' She glanced over at Rosanne, her expression apologetic. 'Though I'm afraid much of this will mean little or nothing to you, Ros, I wanted you here because it might go some way to explaining the many things which must have puzzled you about my attitude to the work you've been doing—and which you've been far too polite to mention.' She paused, her eyes moving from the blank-faced, immobile Rosanne to the man now leaning his head back against the side of her chair. 'I've always accepted that there will eventually have to be at least one—if not more—biography of my late husband. Although he never did achieve the top position, he was prominent among politicians of his day—and since his death I've been approached several times by would-be biographers, all of whom were aware that without my co-operation with private papers they wouldn't get terribly far.'

'And you've always refused their requests,' muttered Damian, his tone edgy.

Hester nodded. 'One of my reasons being that I simply didn't wish there to be a work on him while I was still alive.' She shook her head impatiently as Damian made to interrupt her. 'Not that I'd have read one—just as I've never read his diaries, though I was perfectly free to do so even before he died.'

Rosanne closed her eyes as though by doing so she could miraculously rid herself of the stridently conflicting emotions waging battle within her.

'When I was seventeen I met the love of my life—a man from these parts. He was killed in a hunting accident a year later.'

Damian's head lifted just as Rosanne's eyes flew open, their expressions almost identical in their shock.

'I only mention that,' murmured Hester wryly as she noted their reaction, 'because I recognised a similar love in my daughter all those years later. You know, they say that we Sheridans are capable of absolute and unreserved love only once in our lifetimes.' She gave a small shrug. 'Perhaps they're right. It was a much tamer emotion that I felt for George Cranleigh when I eventually met and married him, and one that was all but destroyed when he had our daughter made a ward of court after she and Paul had run off and got married. You see, despite George's understandable dislike of Paul, I understood that love of theirs—I knew that trying to separate them was not only cruel, but impossible.'

'What do you mean by your husband's understandable dislike of Paul?' blurted out Rosanne, completely oblivious of the harshly warning look her desperate words elicited from Damian.

'It's a rather long story,' sighed Hester. 'You see——'

'And one there's absolutely no need for you to relate,' cut in Damian, flashing Rosanne a blackly murderous look.

'Oh, but there is,' protested Hester gently, placing a restraining hand on his arm. 'George and Paul had clashed on several occasions before Faith ever met the boy. You see, George was Minister of Education at the time and Paul Bryant was up at Cambridge.' She had given deliberate emphasis to the surname, glancing over at Rosanne as she did so. 'Does it surprise you to hear that it was his father who founded the publishing house for which you work?'

Her guard almost completely gone, Rosanne barely knew nor cared what her face might be betraying—all she wanted was for Hester to continue.

'The students had been up in arms for several months over government policies, feeling that the poorer among them would be seriously disadvantaged if certain plans were implemented. Paul was part of a group who made a point of heckling George and generally making life difficult for him whenever he spoke publicly—in fact, behaving the way idealistic young people have always done the world over whenever they feel their principles are threatened. Unfortunately George had forgotten what it was to be young and idealistic and as several of these students, including young Paul, came from moneyed backgrounds, he regarded them as nothing more than trouble-makers.'

'But how did Faith meet him?' asked Damian, now obviously intrigued.

'Quite by chance—at a mutual friend's place,' replied Hester, her voice sounding suddenly very frail. 'Not that George would ever believe it. He got it into his head that young Paul had engineered the meeting—simply to upset him. And he went on insisting that getting at him was the boy's only motive, no matter who tried to reason with him.'

'Hell, he could hardly keep that line going once they'd run off and got married!' exclaimed Damian, while Rosanne sat in a peculiarly frozen silence.

'George refused to see their relationship other than from his own blinkered point of view,' replied Hester, her words almost entirely devoid of expression. 'I left him and came back here to Ireland when he had Faith made a ward of court,' she continued in that same blank voice. 'And when I learned he intended having the marriage annulled I let him know that he would never see me again if he went ahead with it.'

Damian took one of her hands in his, holding it gently to his cheek. 'And you got your way,' he whispered, the words catching in his throat.

Rosanne watched them, tortured by the incoherent thoughts trying to take form in her mind.

'The shallowest of victories,' replied Hester, her voice aching with bitterness. 'I couldn't afford to align myself openly against him in case he went ahead and had the marriage annulled. But I went back to London to try to reason with him—all I wanted for those two poor youngsters to be left in peace. George simply wouldn't hear of it.' Her knuckles gleamed white against the hand still clasped in Damian's as the words seemed to pour from her of their own volition. 'Yet there was a strength and maturity in those two young people that went far beyond their dewy youth,' she whispered as though to herself. 'Despite their cruel separation they managed to make some sort of contact and sorted everything out as best they could between themselves.'

'How?' demanded Damian, unable to mask his growing anger. 'There don't seem to have been any options open to them with Faith still being under age.'

'To them it was only a matter of time before they would be together again; but it was the fact that Faith had been having problems with high blood-pressure from quite early on in her pregnancy that made any rashness on their part impossible. As it was she had to be admitted into a nursing home because of that hypertension, soon after she was made a ward of court, and she remained there for most of the rest of her pregnancy.'

'Paul must have been half out of his mind with worry!' exclaimed Damian hoarsely, while Rosanne remained locked in a thrall of pain, unable to utter a single word.

'Of course he must have been, but that was where their incredible maturity manifested itself,' said Hester, her voice tinged with pride. 'Faith managed to make him see that, despite everything, she was in the best place as far as their baby was concerned . . . she also suggested he get on with his studies—he was in his final year—teasing him that this baby of theirs would be most put out if its father ended up with a poor degree.' Her voice faltered badly, then recovered as pride once more returned to strengthen it. 'They were such passionate, such volatile young people, yet, for the sake of their unborn baby, they acted with a wisdom way beyond their years.'

'And then?' demanded Rosanne, a rasping harshness in her voice as she tried to disengage her mind from the rambling lunacy of its momentary thought that all this had nothing to do with her and that there might, after all, be a happy ending.

'And then, despite the first-class care Faith had been receiving, she went into labour two weeks early—and the baby was stillborn,' replied Hester, her voice breaking completely.

'You don't have to say any more,' rasped Damian, then flashed Rosanne a look of pure fury. 'She already knows the rest.'

Rosanne neither heard his words nor saw his look; her entire being was preoccupied with a single thought. Had this woman who was her grandmother lied ... or had she simply spoken what she believed to be the truth?

'Hessie, it was for this reason that I didn't want you having anything to do with all this raking over of the past!' exclaimed Damian, plainly deeply upset.

'My darling boy, have you forgotten your parents?' asked Hester quietly.

'Of course I haven't,' he protested. 'But——'

'No—they live on in your memories of them and even if you never again mentioned their names those memories would live on in you for as long as you lived.' She gave a soft chuckle when he flashed her a look of exasperated bemusement. 'Damian, after your dear parents died, I became the centre of your life...and you of mine. On the rare occasions George was here before he retired you were guarded and suspicious of him ... if not downright jealous.'

Rosanne noted the minimal lift and fall of his shoulders that greeted that statement. It certainly wasn't a shrug of denial, more the reflex gesture of a man who, from a very early age, had come to regard the exclusive attention of women, no matter what their role, as his right.

'By then George and I were no more than polite strangers who sometimes shared the same roof,' continued Hester.

'But things improved after he retired and began spending more of his time here,' stated Damian, his shrewd eyes unwavering as they studied his elderly relative.

'Oh, we managed to get on well enough on the surface by then,' conceded Hester. 'And did so only because neither of us ever tried to violate the barriers locking out the past... It was the only way we were able to maintain the façade of our non-existent relationship.'

'But your husband,' blurted out Rosanne, breaking her silence and eliciting those vaguely surprised looks from her companions that told her they had almost completely forgotten her presence. 'Did he never make any attempt to break down those barriers?'

Hester hesitated, then shook her head. 'George was never a man to be plagued by self-doubt. Of course he was devastated by Faith's death, but he remained unshakeable in his conviction that he had acted only as any other caring father would have. To him, the only fault was mine—for not having supported him in his convictions as any dutiful wife should have——' She broke off, hesitating again before continuing.

'There was a time—soon after his first stroke—when he intimated in a roundabout way that I should read his diaries.' She gave a bitter laugh. 'For the briefest of moments I actually thought I'd detected a glimmer of remorse in him.' She shook her head angrily. 'His only remorse was that he'd saddled himself with such an undutiful wife... I've the feeling he hoped that, even after all those years, there was an outside chance I could be brought round to seeing how right he'd always been, simply by reading those damned scribblings of his...God, but he was the blind, obstinate old fool!'

'You didn't read them then and you don't have to read them now!' exploded Damian angrily.

'No, I don't,' Hester reassured him. 'That's a task I'm leaving to Ros to deal with. And I'm sure she'll do as thorough a job on them as she did those tedious engagement diaries of his.' She smiled over at Rosanne. 'And once you're finished you can bundle everything up together with your notes and send the lot to Cedric Lamont—and that'll be my wifely duty done!'

'But won't you want to go over my notes first?' asked Rosanne faintly; her head was pounding and she was feeling drained and slightly nauseous.

Hester shook her head, her smile ironic. 'I don't think so, thank you, my dear. Just do the necessary, then pack it all off to Cedric to sort into something.' She turned to Damian. 'Now—how about some lunch? And then it'll be time for James to take me over to Charlie's.'

Damian rose, his eyes troubled as he gazed down at her. He took a breath, as though about to say something, then expelled it with a defeated sigh.

'And George wasn't the only obstinate old fool,' he muttered exasperatedly as he helped the old lady to her feet.

Rosanne watched their slow progress from the room, her body feeling as though it had been welded to the chair and her mind in hopeless turmoil.

It was only once she had lost Grandpa Ted that the terrible need for revenge had been born in her. She had come here fired with hatred and hell-bent on revenge, she told herself numbly... a person her beloved grandfather probably wouldn't have recognised as her. Yet now the woman from whom she had plotted to seek her retribution appeared either to have no knowledge of the crime... or had managed to blot its hideous actuality from her memory.

She rose and followed in their wake, the attaché case containing what she once believed she would have sold her soul to possess standing forgotten on the floor by her grandmother's chair.

CHAPTER SIX

'RIGHT—let's have a look at whatever dark secrets you've unearthed so far!'

Rosanne gave a silent groan of disbelief at the sound of those words, mentally bracing herself as Damian's presence seemed to explode into the office and shatter its tomb-like calm.

'I beg your pardon?' she muttered, stalling as she made a half-hearted attempt to psych herself up before facing him.

'I thought I'd have a look through your efforts with the saintly George's scribblings,' he replied, leaning his tall body against her desk, his gaze coolly impersonal as it flickered over her seated figure. 'You know,' he continued, before giving her a chance to reply, 'the old boy only embarked on his famed philanthropy after Faith's death... Perhaps Hester's wrong and he actually did feel some sort of remorse.'

Rosanne felt a stab of irritation as her mind began scrabbling around in an attempt to adjust to that relatively chatty statement. In the few days since Hester's departure he had been boorish and unbearable whenever their paths had crossed—which had been reduced to the absolute minimum thanks only to her constant and nerve-racking vigilance.

'I'm sure that's something Cedric Lamont will pick up if it's relevant,' she replied, studiously avoiding any eye contact with him. The last time she had looked into his eyes—during the midst of a blazing verbal exchange over something so mind-bogglingly trivial that she couldn't even remember what it was—she had caught a glimpse of his inner agony and had been almost overwhelmed by a need to open her arms to him and offer him whatever comfort she could.

'Bridie tells me I've been behaving like a pig to everyone and that she'll flatten me if I carry on like this,' he announced, almost amiably. 'She pointed out that she and James and the rest of them are just as anxious as I am about Hester . . . and she's right—they are.'

The 'they' rather than 'we' struck Rosanne as especially pointed before she chided herself for being overly sensitive.

'I honestly can't see what you're worried about,' she stated quietly. 'You've heard from her every day since she left, and the people she's with say she's in very good form,' she added, repeating what Bridie had told her.

'She hasn't much longer left . . . she should be here at home,' he muttered, hoisting himself up on the desk and gazing down morosely at the gleaming booted foot he began swinging back and forth.

'Don't you think you're being rather selfish?' she demanded recklessly. She had far too much on her plate as it was, without having to contend with Damian and his black moods. 'Hester wanted to go to Dublin, for heaven's sake! She wanted to be with her friends there—and she's having those tests her doctor wanted her to have.'

'For once in my life I'm not being selfish,' he replied. 'I'm just not entirely convinced she didn't leave here simply because——'

'Damian, do we have to go over all that again?' she cut in exasperatedly. 'What possible difference can it make whether I go through the diaries with her here or while she's in Dublin?' The moment she uttered the words, she saw the difference—and it filled her with a stomach-churning sense of betrayal. She had almost convinced herself that, however impossible it seemed, her grandmother hadn't known of George Cranleigh's terrible deed. But now she realised that it was the old lady's inability to face that deed becoming known, even to an apparent stranger, that had driven Hester away.

'I don't know!' he bellowed at her. 'All I know is that those bloody diaries do something to her... it's almost as though she's afraid of them!'

Rosanne's lips began tightening to an angry line, then relaxed to trembling uncertainty as she wondered what his reaction would be once he learned the appalling truth about his beloved Hester.

'Anyway, I'm sure all this Celtic *angst* must be terribly wearing for a cool English cookie such as yourself,' he said, his tone switching to a patronising drawl. 'Though that's not really fair to the English—some of whose women have been the most delightfully hot-blooded creatures it's been my pleasure to enjoy... not to mention that Irish blood you claim to have sloshing around somewhere in you.'

Her momentary and misplaced anxiety on his behalf killed stone dead by fury, Rosanne rounded on him with hatred blazing in her eyes.

'Get out of here! Just get out of here and leave me alone!'

'Well, that's novel,' he replied with a chuckle, 'ordering a man out of a room in his own house. Or perhaps it was the entire house, not simply this room, you had in mind.' He slid off the desk and drew up a chair beside her. 'Now—let's have a look at what you've done so far.'

Rosanne fought to retain control of her temper, the depressing realisation dawning on her that, since almost the first instant she had arrived here, she had been waging ceaseless battles of one sort or another with herself.

'Damian, I know you're on edge because you're so worried about Hester,' she sighed, wondering how much longer she could go on like this before snapping completely, 'but taking it out on me isn't going to help—it's only going to make things worse.'

'I'm taking nothing out on you. Just give me those damned papers!'

'Why?' she exploded. 'Hester's no longer here, so what's the point in keeping up this ridiculous charade?'

'What charade?' he growled. 'I'm simply curious to see what you've come up with.'

'Right—if you're curious, I suggest you read the lot for yourself!' she hissed, dragging open one of the drawers and hauling on to the desk the eight five-year diaries which had become the bane of her life.

He glanced over at the leather-bound books, only the first four of which Rosanne had managed to force herself into reading and annotating, an expression close to distaste flickering across his handsome features.

'I'm not that curious,' he drawled, his look baleful as it switched to her. 'When did he start on these?' he demanded suddenly, the unexpectedness of the questioning throwing her.

'When he first entered parliament—about three years before he and Hester got married,' she replied woodenly.

And even then, as a youngish man, there had been a rigidity in him that had leapt from those neatly written pages and chilled her, she reflected bitterly; everything was neatly compartmentalised, everything either black or white, as though no shade of grey had ever existed in that sterile, ordered world.

'So, tell me—what's your opinion of the great man now?'

Rosanne leaned back in her chair as she searched for an answer. It had taken all the mental strength she possessed to steel herself even to open the first of those diaries. Her unacknowledged dread had been finding him not to be the monster of her nightmares. Only by telling herself that she would deal with each in strictly chronological order—and reminding herself that all she had to do was stop if it became too much for her—was she able to make a start.

'I'm not sure . . . he was an incredibly contained man,' she replied with guarded understatement. It had come as both a shock and a comfort to her to find nothing about him reaching out to appeal to her.

'You mean he was a cold, unyielding bastard,' retorted Damian with his customary candour. 'God, only a Sheridan would be perverse enough to take on a character like that!' he exclaimed exasperatedly. 'Though, I suppose, if you've lost the one true love of your life, as Hester had, a challenge as big as George would have had some perverse sort of appeal.'

'I've a feeling he might have regarded her as some sort of a challenge too,' mused Rosanne. 'I mean—marrying someone as vibrantly different as Hester obviously was seemed so completely out of character for him. Perhaps he loved her desperately,' she added without much conviction.

'I take it, from the "perhaps", that there wasn't any passionate poet to be found lurking behind that smugly self-righteous exterior?' he murmured drily.

Rosanne gave a wan smile as she shook her head. 'No, I'm afraid he comes over as cold on paper as he apparently did in life—despite his later philanthropy. But you were right about the political details. In many instances he's recorded his opponents' entire cases—which might seem very generous of him until you read on and realise that, no matter how good the argument against him, his was the only valid view as far as he was concerned.'

'No, it didn't pay to cross that opinionated old devil,' muttered Damian bitterly. 'As Paul Bryant learned to his cost.' He hesitated momentarily, then continued. 'And what about Faith—no glimmer of self-doubt in him over her?' he demanded grimly.

Rosanne was conscious of every muscle in her body tightening up painfully.

'I . . . I haven't got that far,' she muttered, then began rummaging around in one of the drawers as though searching for something vital.

And she was honestly beginning to think she never would get that far, she admitted to herself with a sick, stomach-churning feeling of desolation. It had taken more out of her than she had ever dreamed possible, reading through those years that had covered her mother's brief life—here and there gleaning the odd snippet of childhood achievements and misdemeanours as penned, often with undoubted love, by that essentially cold and inhibited father.

She gave a startled cry as she felt her hands drawn away from the drawer and her body pushed back gently against the chair. She hadn't even heard Damian move, but now he was on his feet and gazing down at her with an expression that puzzled her even as it started up the inevitable racing of her pulses.

'You're right, I am a selfish devil!' he exclaimed softly.

Rosanne gazed up at him in hot-cheeked bemusement, waiting for an explanatory expansion of that startling admission.

'Come on,' he said briskly, taking her by the hand and drawing her up from the chair. 'Let's go and have ourselves a drink.'

Now what? Rosanne asked herself in complete bewilderment as she followed him down the hallway and into the misnamed blue drawing-room, the warmth of the hand still enclosing hers sending jolts of tingling awareness up her arm and through her body.

Her eyes travelled up the length of his body, savouring its tall perfection and lingering at the back of his neck, where darkly gleaming hair with an unruly hint of curl merged with the black polo-neck of his sweater.

She had never been in love, she thought—as though that were the most natural topic for her to be thinking right at that very moment. A couple of times she had been in love with the idea of being in love, and had enjoyed the exhilarating excitement of it all. She shivered as she suddenly thought of the sort of love her parents had shared and was perturbed by the vague sense of apprehension the thought had awakened in her. Then her eyes rose, catching Damian's profile as he turned slightly to open the door, and the apprehension within her sharpened into focus. Faults and all, this man was the prince her heart had awaited, she realised with a sickeningly plummeting heart, and she had virtually recognised him as such from the first instant she had set eyes on him.

'Right—what would you like to drink?' he asked once he had got her seated in front of the fire. 'Whiskey? Brandy? Gin perhaps?'

'I don't really drink spirits,' she protested, her mind in a daze of apprehensive confusion and suspicion. Why on earth was he suddenly fussing over her like this?

'Well, I'm prescribing a brandy,' he announced, then frowned as he scrutinised her. 'Are you sure you're warm enough? You look all pinched and peaky.'

Tact was certainly not one of his stronger points, thought Rosanne, and she was thrown to find herself reacting with a rush of affectionate amusement.

'I'm fine,' she muttered, feeling edgy and peculiarly threatened.

She watched as he walked over to the drinks cabinet at the far corner of the room, angrily remonstrating with herself to forget about fairy-tales of princes and knights on white chargers and to start behaving like the rational human being she was... or had been until she had set foot in this place, she corrected herself despondently.

'I've only given you a smidgen,' he promised, returning with two brandy balloons and passing her one before sitting down beside her. 'Slàinte,' he murmured, raising his glass.

'Was that Irish?' she asked, the words staggering clumsily off her tongue as she strove to sound composed.

'It was,' he replied, rolling his glass between his palms while his eyes held hers in the gentlest of mockery.

Mortified to feel the colour rushing to her cheeks and with the vague thought running through her mind that she had heard brandy had calming properties, she took a reckless gulp from her glass. She then spent the next several seconds concentrating her every effort on not choking as her throat put up violent objections to the fiery ball being propelled down it.

'I think you'll find it slides down a lot easier if you take it a sip at a time,' observed Damian, his amused tone destroying any remaining shred of her composure.

'Would you mind telling me what all this is in aid of?' she demanded coldly, depositing her glass on the small table beside her and vowing not to touch another drop of its contents.

'All what?'

'For heaven's sake, you know perfectly well what I mean!' she snapped, infuriated by that drawling tone. 'One minute you're being your usual unpleasant self and the next you've dragged me in here and started treating me as though I'm some sort of invalid!'

'My usual unpleasant self?' he echoed in tones of pained disbelief. His hand reached out and turned her face towards his, an expression of seriousness settling over his features. 'Ros, do you honestly think I'm so cold-hearted that I wouldn't have understood?' he asked quietly.

For one terrible moment her mind froze.

'Understood what?' she croaked.

'Damn it, Ros, why do you insist on keeping up this ridiculous act?' he demanded, impatience creeping into his tone. 'Do you think I wasn't aware of the way you were affected by what Hester told us the day she left and the fight you were putting up not to let it show?'

Rosanne now felt as though every functioning part of her body had turned to lead despite the voice of re-assurance crying out in her that there was no way he could possibly have uncovered her secret.

'So why can't you simply admit that, far from your being the hard-hearted bitch you're so intent on making yourself out to be, there's a tenderness in you that balks at the thought of going through the next phase of those diaries on your own? Hell, your reaction is perfectly normal—it's the most tragic of stories!'

Rosanne half turned towards him, a peculiar choking sound escaping her as, giddy with relief, she attempted taking in a huge gulp of air just as her beleaguered lungs began expelling their fill.

His reaction was a soft groan of exasperation before he put an arm around her and drew her head against his shoulder.

'You're just about the most perplexing woman it's ever been my misfortune to meet,' he sighed. 'Why the hell didn't you tell me how it was getting to you? Surely you don't think I'd not have understood?'

Rosanne was barely hearing his words. Her relief was being rapidly dissipated by the memory of his teasing threat once to have her investigated and the sickening realisation of how little investigation it would take to uncover the fact that she had been acknowledged as Edward Bryant's granddaughter both during his life and in his will; that her name had been changed by deed poll from Grant—under which she was now masquerading—to Bryant; and that she was co-owner of the publishing house bearing that name. In fact, she realised with mounting panic, all he had to do was pick up a phone and ring Bryant's to find they had no knowledge of any Ros Grant!

It was the sensation of Damian's hand stroking absent-mindedly against her hair that began diluting her panic with feelings of utter despair. One day soon he would know the true reasons for her having come here . . . and then he would despise her.

'Ros, I don't relish the thought of it any more than you do,' he said. 'But tomorrow we'll tackle it together.'

'No!' As that single word of rejection exploded from her she was drawing from him in agitation. 'No,' she repeated with less force, stunned to her senses by his look of wary bemusement. 'Damian, it's very sweet of you to offer——'

'It wasn't in the least *sweet* of me,' he cut in with disparaging emphasis. 'I want all this dealt with and the lot dumped in Cedric Lamont's lap as soon as humanly possible, so that Hester can come home where she belongs.'

Hester, thought Rosanne bitterly; his considerations, as always, were only for his beloved Hester.

'I understand that,' she replied with quiet resolve. 'And that's the job I'm here to do.'

'But one you haven't been able to carry out so far,' he pointed out accusingly.

'Damian, there's a limit to how fast I can work!' she exclaimed with forced brightness. 'I've covered four of the diaries since Hester left—a period of twenty years, in case it had escaped your notice.'

'Oh, no, it hadn't escaped my notice,' he replied, locking his hands at the back of his neck and tilting his head back against them. 'In fact, I was most impressed at the speed with which you'd covered that daunting stretch of time...or I was the day before yesterday, when I was in the study and had a look through what you'd achieved.'

Rosanne closed her eyes as though praying for inspiration. Apart from launching into an attack and accusing him of spying on her—an idea she immediately rejected as dangerously unwise—she could think of nothing.

'So—what brought you to so abrupt a halt?' he demanded harshly.

'I...it's just that I got a bit carried away with the diaries at first. Well, very carried away, to be frank——' She broke off, willing herself to moderate the gabbled speed of the words suddenly pouring from her. 'I must have overdone it. Mr Cranleigh's writing is small, even though it is so neat, but I decided it was time I took a break when I started having difficulties reading it.'

'Perhaps you should get your eyes tested,' he suggested, no shred of sympathy in his tone.

Rosanne shook her head. 'There's really no need for that. As I said, I got carried away and overdid things,' she said with forced brightness, while inwardly cringing from how repetitive and unconvincing she sounded. 'I'll be ready to plough on again tomorrow.'

'Good—I look forward to joining you,' he said, lowering his arms and bestowing the most stunning of smiles on her.

Rosanne's heart plummeted.

'Damian, that simply isn't necessary,' she protested. 'And, apart from everything else, you haven't the training to do this sort of thing.'

'Training?' he enquired, his eyes icy. 'Ros, I'd be grateful if you'd credit me with at least a little intelligence. I may have next to no idea what goes on in publishing houses, but I'm darned sure the dreary legwork you've been asked to do here isn't normal procedure. So don't give me any more rubbish about the lengthy training required to carry out a task any literate clerk could handle with ease. And don't try telling me two of us couldn't finish this off more quickly than one.'

'Well, I don't think we could,' she retorted exasperatedly. 'And besides, you have your stables to run—you wouldn't have the time.'

'That's just where you're wrong,' he replied smugly. 'It's about time Joe and the lads had a practice run at looking after the place on their own.'

'Why have you suddenly decided there's a need for them to be able to run the place without you?' asked Rosanne, determined to change the subject no matter how barefaced her attempt would appear.

'I could give you a dozen reasons,' he replied, his look of mocking amusement taunting her with his awareness of her blatant ploy. 'One of them being that I'll probably be going down to Dublin soon.'

'To check on Hester,' burst out Rosanne exasperatedly before she had a chance to stop herself.

'No, not to check on her—to be with her.'

Rosanne's eyes flew to his face, drawn by something indefinable in his voice. There was that same proud aloofness in his features, but there were shadows too that seemed to tell of an inner despair. And it was because what she saw on his face reawakened memories in her of the savage desolation that had racked her when she had first realised she was about to lose her beloved grandfather that she reached over and placed her hand on his arm in a spontaneous gesture of comfort.

He turned his head, lowering it as he gazed down at the hand on his arm, a slight tremor seeming to shiver

through his body as he then placed his own hand over
hers.

Rosanne found herself guiltily wondering at her own
selfish stupidity. She had immediately seen, and even
envied, the very special love between Damian and Hester,
yet she had never taken into consideration the terrible
torment he must be suffering at the knowledge that he
must soon lose the woman who had been a mother and
so much more to him.

'Damian, I——' She broke off with a gasp of disbelief
as she realised that the emotion she had so fancifully
imagined to be racking him right at this very moment
was no more than the laughter that he was so unsuc-
cessfully trying to suppress. 'Perhaps you'd care to share
this hilarious joke,' she hissed indignantly as he gave up
his struggle and dissolved into full-throated laughter.

'Why, the devious old bissom,' he choked, plainly still
finding whatever it was excruciatingly funny. 'I've just
thought of another reason why Hester was so eager to
hare off to Dublin.'

As he went into another paroxysm of laughter,
Rosanne irritably tried to snatch away her hand, only to
find that he wasn't quite so overcome by mirth not to
be capable of stopping her by entwining his long, tanned
fingers firmly around hers.

'Perhaps—once you've recovered—you'll get around
to telling me what all this is about,' she muttered, but
she was already battling against the infectious effect of
his laughter.

'I'm sorry,' he began, still obviously struggling to
compose himself. 'You see——' One glance at her told
him of the effect he was having on her and the rest of
his words dissolved into deep-throated chuckles.

'Damian Sheridan, you really are the most irritating
man I've ever met,' groaned Rosanne through her own
laughter.

'Irritating?' he choked indignantly.

She nodded, the laughter suddenly dying in her as she accepted that she would protect his relationship with Hester no matter what it cost her... and that she would do so because there was no other word for the confusion and torment of her feelings towards him but love.

'Irritating, be damned!' he whispered huskily, all laughter gone from him as he drew her towards him, lifting her imprisoned hand to nestle at the curve of his neck before he drew her fully into his arms. 'If there's only one thing I've ever been completely sure of with you, it's that you want me every bit as much as I want you,' he murmured hotly against her lips.

'Damian, I——'

'And if you try to deny it, I'll break every rib in this tempting little body of yours,' he threatened with teasing confidence, his arms tightening suffocatingly around her. 'But what I've never been able to understand is why wanting me should frighten you as it so obviously does.'

There was a sweetly melting tenderness in his lips as they parted hers, as though to convince her there was no need to be afraid. And she clung to him, her lips answering his with a fearless abandon that she was powerless to temper despite the shock of the resistance she momentarily encountered in him. Then he gave a softly groaned growl of defeat, his arms lifting her against him, an impatient hunger replacing the tender gentleness of his kisses.

There was a part of her that seemed to hold back, more intrigued than shocked by her careless abandonment of herself to emotions she had never before experienced. Then even that one part of her became lost as his hands began roaming her body, awakening ever more powerful and urgent longings within her as they impatiently pushed aside any barrier they encountered to explore and caress against her skin. Almost as though it was second nature to them, her own hands began their reciprocal exploration, the sharp jolts of excitement piercing through her becoming heightened by a heady sense of an incredible power when she felt the silken smoothness beneath her hands contract in instant response to her touch.

'What are you doing to me, Ros?' he groaned, lifting his head and gazing down at her from eyes that were soft and sleepy yet burned with an inner depth of passion.

She gazed up at him, her breath catching in her throat as she tried to speak but was rendered incapable by the exquisite torture his hands continued to inflict on her now violently trembling body. And as their eyes remained locked she felt the hot surge of passion that leapt in his body and the response her own body gave brought a ragged cry of need from him as he lowered his head to the hollow of her throat and began bathing it in soft, murmuring kisses.

This was what loving meant, she rejoiced as her arms cradled him possessively against her. As her mother had before her loved her father, so she would love this man till eternity.

'Ros?' he whispered hoarsely, again raising his head as he sensed the sudden tension in her.

She was shaking her head, even as her arms clung even tighter around him, trying to blot out the stark reality blasting its way into her consciousness. 'Damian, I——'

'I know, darling,' he whispered unevenly, then drew completely away from her. He took a couple of steadying breaths before continuing. 'I promise you, it wasn't my intention to leap on you and ravish you like a slavering maniac.' He gave her a rueful, slightly dazed smile that sent her heart lurching into a series of violent somersaults. 'It just kind of turned out that way.'

'I have to disagree most strongly with the slavering maniac bit,' she said, attempting to joke but ending up uttering words that were simply breathless and distorted. 'But I think I understand what you mean.'

She gazed down at her hands, clenched tightly in her lap to mask their trembling, the stupefying realisation of her hopeless position engulfing her like a dank shroud. The one man she had chosen to love was the one man whom she had known, from almost the moment she had met him, would one day hate her.

'You seem to be having second thoughts,' he murmured wryly, breaking the silence hanging heavily between them.

She lifted her head and looked over at him, a half-forgotten memory springing unexpectedly to her mind.

She shook her head, partly in reply to him and partly to tell herself that the memory shouldn't have been all that unexpected.

'I was thinking of something that happened to me ages ago,' she said quietly, and immediately wondered what had possessed her to mention it.

'Well?'

'It was nothing really,' she muttered awkwardly, feeling she had no option but to continue. 'What I thought was to be a straightforward goodnight kiss got rather out of hand.'

'Rather in the way my good-afternoon kiss did just now?' he enquired, a chill edge in his tone.

She shook her head, almost squirming with embarrassment. 'You see, the other man got very nasty and accused me of leading him on—which I hadn't. You, on the other hand, didn't get in the least nasty...and, well...' Her words petered to a stammered halt.

'You had been leading me on?'

'Would you mind if we changed the subject?' she snapped, angered and hurt by his drawling sarcasm.

'Yes, I do mind,' he retorted, settling himself back comfortably against the sofa and stretching his long legs out before him in total relaxation. 'I think I've already mentioned that I'm never led anywhere I don't want to be led. And I've no time whatever for men who complain of women leading them on—all they're really doing is proclaiming their own lack of self-control.' He turned and gave her a look which she found most disturbingly predatory. 'And, before you get any ideas about nominating me for a sainthood, I should remind you that, from the start, I've made my intentions towards you as plain as any man possibly can. The only reason I was so ready to stop before things got really out of hand just now is that I didn't relish the idea of giving poor Bridie a fit of the vapours—which is probably what she'd have had if she'd walked in on us in the throes of lovemaking.'

Rosanne felt as if she had just had a bucket of cold water flung over her. Here she was, having a mental crisis over having made the worst choice possible to love . . . while the object of all her *angst* sprawled in total relaxation beside her and referred to the prospect of making love to her with as much emotion as he would discussing his next meal!

'Well, bully for you,' she practically spat at him, and felt like breaking something over his head when he responded with laughter. 'Which reminds me,' she continued coldly. 'Before you go into another bout of convulsions, perhaps you'd be so good as to tell me what brought on the first.'

'I thought I already had,' he murmured enigmatically, his eyes twinkling in a manner that left her feeling decidedly uneasy. 'I've already mentioned Hester's matchmaking ambitions on my behalf. Well, I'm not for a moment suggesting that leaving us alone here was her only reason for haring off to Dublin . . . but I'm sure the idea made going all that more attractive.'

'Very funny,' muttered Rosanne.

'What's funny about it?' he asked innocently. 'She's always had my interests at heart—even though I've tended to laugh at her machinations. To be absolutely honest, I've never much fancied any of the women she's lined up for me.'

Rosanne gave him a surreptitious look, just to check that he actually was joking. She looked away, none the wiser.

'But I got to thinking—perhaps in my stubbornness I'd been cutting off my nose to spite my face in rejecting them simply because they were Hester's choice for me.'

'Oh, I see,' said Rosanne, completely unable to believe her ears. 'So you thought you'd take a closer look at me—in order to give Hester the benefit of the doubt?'

'Let's face it, darling,' he replied easily, 'I'd already started looking pretty intently at you from the moment you arrived. I suppose I was—in a manner of speaking— having a go at killing two birds with one stone.'

'That closer look you were giving me,' murmured Rosanne with sickly sweetness, 'was that as a prospective bedmate for you, or as a prospective bride for Hester's sake?'

'Does it really matter which?' he drawled, his eyes responding in kind to the frigid hostility in hers.

'No—not really, Damian,' she replied, getting to her feet. 'Except that I suggest you and Hester select some other poor fool on which to experiment—I don't wish to take part in the trial.'

'Yet you seemed to be taking part with such enthusiasm not so long ago,' he drawled.

'Yes, I was,' she conceded—she could hardly do otherwise, she reminded herself bitterly. 'But, no matter how physically attractive I find a man, I draw the line at entering into a relationship with him simply to oblige another woman—even if that woman is as near as damn it his mother.'

'Oh, dear, Hester will be disappointed,' he murmured, but there was a decided scowl on his features.

Rosanne turned and marched towards the door. There was a dam inside her about to erupt at any moment and she wanted to be as far away as possible from Damian Sheridan when it happened.

'By the way, Ros,' his drawling words floated after her. 'I expect to see you in the study at nine sharp tomorrow morning—we have a lot of work to get through.'

CHAPTER SEVEN

AFTER a night comprising intermittent bouts of half-sleep, Rosanne eventually awoke late and exhausted. Her hair still damp from a shower that had done little to refresh her, she flew down to the dining-room and helped herself to coffee.

'You look as though you could do with a good fry in you,' chided Bridie, who had bustled in after her. 'Did you not sleep too well?'

'I didn't sleep that well,' admitted Rosanne with a wan smile. 'But all I need is a couple of cups of this,' she said, indicating the coffee.

'That stuff will do you no good,' muttered Bridie. 'But, if that's all you're having, I'll make you up a fresh pot of it.'

Rosanne shook her head, glancing down at her watch as she did. 'That's sweet of you, Bridie, honestly, but this is fine. And besides, I've an appointment with Damian in the study at nine.'

'An appointment, indeed?' chuckled the house-keeper, and said no more. But there was a twinkle in her eyes as she cleared the breakfast things from the table and later she paused on her way out of the room to give an archly bemused shake of her head before leaving.

No doubt Hester had an ally in Bridie when it came to her matchmaking plans, thought Rosanne irritably, and, knowing Hester, she probably consulted the house-keeper—and also her husband, James, for all she knew—on the suitability of potential mates for their darling Damian!

She drained her cup and poured herself another, wondering how she would possibly get through this day while at the same time wondering at the rubbish that had flitted through her mind during those ghastly hours of the night. There was a point at which she had decided she was cursed—and had obviously derived some deranged comfort from the fact, because it was after that point that she had fallen into her last and longest bout of sleep!

She poured herself a third cup of coffee, telling herself that being cursed was as logical an answer as any as to why an otherwise relatively sane woman would find herself in love with a man she positively hated at times.

She made her almost stumbling way to the study, telling herself that, if she didn't clear her head of all this airy-fairy nonsense about princes and cursed maidens, she'd be a prime case for being certified.

'You're almost one minute late,' came Damian's greeting the moment she entered the room.

He was standing at the window with his back to her, dressed in dark, well-fitting trousers and a pale blue sweater... and all she wanted to do was turn and run as the love—which she now realised she had secretly been praying was only a hideous figment of her imagination—washed over her in huge, crushing waves.

'Only joking,' he said, turning and grinning at her.

She tried to smile, but found her facial muscles frozen into rigidity, then, for one ghastly moment, she felt as though she were about to be sick.

'My God, you look awful!' exclaimed Damian, a disconcertingly cheery note in his voice as he strode towards her. 'Do you not feel well—is that why you weren't down for breakfast?'

For an instant her mind grappled with trying to concoct an oncoming illness of such magnitude that he would call an ambulance that would carry her away from all her troubles.

'I overslept,' she muttered defeatedly, the only words that came with any intelligibility to her mind.

'You'd better go and have some breakfast—you look as though you're about to fade away.'

'I've had all the breakfast I want,' she replied, walking to the desk.

'OK—so let's get to work, then,' he said, drawing up a chair and flinging himself down on it. 'I'm in your hands entirely—I've no idea how we go about this.'

Rosanne sat down, trying to suppress a shuddering sigh as one of the major points plaguing her during the night returned to torment her once more.

'Damian, I honestly thought you were joking yesterday,' she pleaded. No matter what her past sins, Hester meant the world to him—and, because he was now her entire world, she would move heaven and earth to spare him this pain. 'Anyway, there's no way I can work with you breathing down my neck.'

'Something tells me you lied to me, Ros,' he stated quietly. 'And that you have read through the diaries.'

'Oh, for heaven's sake——'

'Just who the hell do you think you are?' he cut harshly through her words. 'Some sort of nanny, protecting me from the naughty deeds of someone only on the fringes of my family?'

She wanted to rant at him—accuse him of paranoia, then realised with a sickening certainty that no matter how she carried on he would insist on having his way and that the contents of the diaries, for which she no longer had any stomach, would be laid bare.

'Damian, I didn't lie to you,' she said instead, and guilt over all the other lies she actually had told him rose like bitter bile in her throat. 'I've only read the four diaries I've worked on.'

He shrugged, then leaned back in his chair. 'OK—so how do we go about tackling the next four?'

They opted for his reading the entries out to her, while she made notes on the word processor.

The first half of that fifth diary which had so repelled her turned out to contain far more political intrigue now that George Cranleigh had reached cabinet status.

'My, this should cause a few red faces even now,' Damian chuckled at one point.

And, as she listened to his softly lilting voice and sometimes laughed at his wickedly barbed asides, Rosanne was almost lulled into believing that no horror would ever unfold.

At the very first mention of her father's name she froze and it was several seconds before she became aware that Damian had stopped reading.

'Poor devil,' he muttered, suddenly depositing the leather-bound diary on the desk in a gesture of disgust. 'To be perfectly frank, this is beginning to give me the creeps!'

Rosanne kept her eyes trained on the keyboard before her.

'Why don't you just call it a day?' she suggested, striving to keep her tone neutral. 'Now that we're into it, I shan't have any problems continuing on my own.'

There was a pause which she found intensely nerve-racking before he finally spoke.

'You're admitting you weren't that happy about it before, are you?'

Rosanne gave a small shrug of defeat; she would only tie herself up in knots by trying to retract her careless admission. She felt too drained even to feel relief when he didn't press his point.

'What I suggest we do now,' he continued, 'is have a break for lunch. Afterwards, I think it would be better to read through the entire Faith and Paul episode from beginning to end. It's something so far removed from all this political stuff that I'm sure it's better to have the whole picture before you start rendering it into notes.'

With shaking hands, Rosanne turned off the machine as he got to his feet. That afternoon they were to render her parents' passionate young lives into a few compact notes, she thought dazedly to herself, and once again the terrible churning within her left her on the verge of being physically sick.

There was an edgy tension in him after lunch, though Rosanne couldn't be entirely sure that it wasn't her mind projecting her own sickening dread on to him.

'I never expected to feel quite like this about coming face to face with it,' he told her in unexpected confirmation of the strain she had suspected. 'I suppose it's because it's something that's always hovered around the fringes of my life, yet I've never really known any of the details ... do you understand what I mean?'

'Of course I do,' she said; but that was all she said, knowing that she would only be wasting her breath making any more attempt to dissuade him.

'But do you understand Hester's not wanting to hear George's side of it?' he exclaimed bitterly. 'Because I do! And surely even you must too! From what you've read so far, it doesn't take much imagination to realise what a self-righteous, cold-hearted swine he was.'

A picture of her Grandpa Ted leapt to her mind: easygoing and exuding love ... the complete antithesis of her maternal grandfather.

'We'll take it all into the drawing-room—we might as well do it in a bit of comfort,' he said, rising from the lunch table.

He seemed irritated by Rosanne's decision to bring a notepad and pen with her, but she stood her ground, knowing there might come a point when she would need something simply to occupy her already shaking hands.

But her ordeal turned out to be far worse than any-thing she could have imagined, exacerbated by Damian's tendency to become so incensed by what was unfolding before his eyes that he would curse angrily to himself, then continue reading in silence.

'Faith and young Bryant just didn't stand a chance!' he exclaimed bitterly at one point. 'George had him singled out from that group of students right from the start.'

He lapsed into silence as he read on.

'For heaven's sake, Damian, how many times do I have to tell you not to do that?' exclaimed Rosanne edgily, glaring over at the form sprawled on the sofa and wondering how long it would be before she snapped completely.

For a long period he restrained himself and from be-tween the lines of her grandfather's coldly biased words Rosanne could almost feel the indomitable strength of her parents' love reaching out towards her. But as he read on she felt the words begin twisting into her heart until all she wanted was to cry out for him to stop.

When he next fell silent she offered no word of protest. Then, as the silence grew, she forced her eyes over to the figure of the man on the sofa and her heart cried out in love to him as she saw the deathly pallor of his features and knew that he was at last learning the ter-rible truth from which she had tried in vain to protect him.

'Dear God—no!' he exploded in an agonised groan. 'The evil, vindictive bastard!' The diary dropped from his hands, slid across his body and hit the floor. 'There *was* a child—a daughter,' he said, his voice lowering to a hoarse whisper. 'She lived!'

Rosanne's hands gripped the arms of the chair to prevent herself running to him to offer what comfort she could.

'Did you hear what I said?' he said, rage choking his words. 'Faith and Paul's child *lived*! And that bastard had it farmed out for adoption when it had parents who wanted it as much as any child could ever be wanted! When it had a grandmother—hell, no, *two* grand-mothers and a grandfather... He cheated Hester and the Bryants of——'

'Hester!' cut in Rosanne, horrified by the harshness in her voice. 'Why didn't she stop him?'

He sat up, his eyes dark with disbelief as they glared over at her. 'Do you think she wouldn't have moved heaven and earth to had she known? Dear God, she——' He broke off, slumping back down against the cushions. 'Read it for yourself,' he muttered wearily.

Rosanne gazed over at the diary lying on the floor beside him, her look that of one both repelled and fas-cinated. It wasn't true, she protested over and over to herself before the silent chant within her was arrested by the realisation that, from the first day she had met her maternal grandmother, she had been filled with an ob-sessive need to hear exactly what it was that she was now so mindlessly rejecting. Propelled to her feet by the un-bearable thought that Damian might be mistaken, she went over to him, forcing herself to pick up the dis-carded diary as she knelt down beside the sofa.

As she read the man beside her poured out a dis-jointed litany of curses against the man he had disliked in life and now hated with a murderous intensity in death.

When she had finished reading, the diary slid from her hands back to the floor and of the myriad tortured thoughts besieging her mind the clearest was of how ashamed her beloved grandfather would be of the ways she had gone about unearthing the truth. With no facts to go on, other than George Cranleigh's guilt, he had been too decent a person to leap to any conclusions that might prove unjust regarding Hester. He had opened the way for her to find the truth, had she so wished . . . but he would never have dreamed she would go about it in the vengeful, underhand manner she had.

She thought of Hester, her witty, kind, lovable grandmother, and the last remnants of the ice shrouding her heart melted with love.

'Thank God she never read them,' Damian said suddenly, breaking into her tortured reverie. 'Perhaps some protective sixth sense warned her not to...but, whatever, thank God she didn't.'

Rosanne looked down at him, trying desperately to clear her mind to make way for comprehension of his words.

'Why do you say that?' she asked uncertainly, and only then felt the shock waves of the past few minutes begin bombarding her.

'I'd have thought it was perfectly obvious why,' he growled, his gaze hostile as it met hers.

'But she'll have to know,' she protested dazedly. She would have to know that she had a granddaughter who loved her!

'You think I'm trying to play God as usual, don't you?' he accused, dragging himself upright and swinging his feet down on to the floor. 'But try putting yourself in Hester's place. You'd have to go far to find someone with her laid-back attitude to her own approaching death.'

Rosanne bit frantically into her bottom lip as she tried not to flinch from those words.

'But how do you think she'd feel, knowing how little time she has left and suddenly finding out there's a granddaughter of hers out there who probably doesn't even know of her existence?' Damian went on. 'How do you think she'd feel, knowing that tracking down that granddaughter would take longer than she has left? And, believe me, it would.'

'Damian, I——' She broke off, willing herself to find the words to tell him the truth while every part of her recoiled from the very thought of it. Even now the open hostility in his eyes was more than she could bear... meeting his hatred face to face would destroy her. 'You asked me to put myself in...in Hester's place,' she whispered hoarsely. 'If I were her, I'd have to know.'

He rose, his expression a disturbing mixture of anger and desolation as he looked down at her.

'Obviously it wasn't such a great idea—asking someone like you to try to put herself in Hester's place,' he stated coldly.

Rosanne's eyes were trained on the floor beside her as those deliberately insulting words hit her ears. She watched in silence as his foot nudged tentatively against the discarded diary, then heard the expletive blasting from him as his foot swung back and kicked the book across the room.

She might just as well have told him, for all the difference it would have made, she told herself with a sudden weariness that was almost detachment as she heard him walk away and the door close behind him. This accursed love she felt for him, which she had once even had the temerity to compare to her parents' unique love, had never for one moment stood a chance of being returned. Damian Sheridan would probably never have given her so much as the time of day had fate not shoved her right under his nose.

She leaned back on her heels, her face curiously expressionless as she remembered their first meeting, then the devastating intensity of the attraction that had flared between them when he had kissed her.

She rose to her feet, retrieved the diary and placed it with the others. Perhaps that devastating attraction had been mutual—perhaps not. And perhaps there might have been a chance of his one day loving that carefree

person her beloved grandfather had released in her during
those brief, love-filled months...but all the perhapses
in the world couldn't change the way things were; nor
the fact that the one thing she could never bring herself
to face was seeing hatred burning in his eyes. And, because she couldn't face what she knew to be inevitable,
she knew the day would soon come when she would never
be able to look into those beloved eyes again.

She picked up the diaries and returned to the study,
her actions those of an automaton as she sat down and
switched on the word processor.

It wasn't even as though she had to spend hours ag-
onising over what to do, she reminded herself—it was
all quite clear-cut and simple. She would finish her work
here, because that was what she knew her grandmother
would want. Then she would leave for Dublin... For
several moments she sat absolutely still, willing herself
not to break. Then she would go to Dublin and put her
arms around that frail figure and tell her the truth...
But once she had left she would never see Damian again.

CHAPTER EIGHT

'Ros, what the hell do you think you're doing? It's way past midnight!'

From the corner of her eye Rosanne could see Damian standing in the doorway. She turned her head slightly so that she no longer could, her fingers flying manically over the keyboard.

'Bridie thought you'd gone out somewhere when you didn't show up for dinner—she was worried about you.'

She made a mental note to apologise to Bridie, then carried on with her work. It was like a glue holding her together—if she stopped she would fall apart.

'Ros?'

'I want to get this finished,' she muttered, praying he would go away. 'What have you done?' she shrieked, panic in her voice as the screen before her suddenly went blank.

'I've pulled out the damned plug,' he replied. 'Ros, what the hell's got into you? This is crazy!'

'How dare you do that?' she raged. 'You could have damaged my word processor!'

'If I have, I'll get you another one,' he retorted dismissively, jamming his fists into the pockets of his dark, heavy silk robe as he strode to her side and scowled down at her. 'Is that all you can think of?' he demanded harshly. 'That bloody machine and your precious work? Though your work's never struck me as being particularly important to you before.'

'Just go away and leave me alone!'

121

His reply was to grab her by the arms and yank her to her feet.

'Are you completely devoid of compassion that you can just carry on as though nothing of any importance has happened?' he raged. 'Have you——?' He broke off with an angry groan, his mouth bruising against hers in impassioned punishment as he pulled her against him.

It was only when she discovered the terrible tension that seemed to tauten every muscle of his lithe body that she realised how instinctively her arms had reached out to embrace him.

'I don't understand you,' he groaned against her softly compliant mouth. 'I've tried to, but I can't. All I know is that I want you as I've never wanted anyone in my life before. Ros, I——'

'It doesn't matter,' she whispered, silencing his tortured outburst with the melting tenderness of her own kiss.

She could use whatever ploy she wanted to occupy her tormented mind, but she would never escape the fact that this was the man she loved, and if he needed her—no matter that it be a need in which love played no part—she would answer him and no power on earth would stop her.

'This is one of the many things I can't find any explanation for in you,' he protested huskily, 'this confusing blend of ice and fire... don't revert to being an ice maiden on me, Ros.'

'I shan't,' she promised, the vow choking out of her in a gasp as his hands began moving with a compulsive restlessness against her body, stirring the fires already kindled in her to a blazing heat.

He removed her arms from where they clung around his waist, replacing them around his neck.

'Hold on tight,' he whispered, then picked her up in his arms.

She held fast to him, burying her face against the warmth of his neck and absorbing the spiced, heady scent of him while his mouth nuzzled against her cheek in murmuring caress.

The door of his room was open and it was the light from just a single bedside lamp that cast its limpid, candle-like glow across the rumpled darkness of the bed.

He returned her to her feet, his gaze never once leaving hers as he kicked the door shut behind them. For one brief instant their eyes remained locked then they fell on one another, straining to touch and to explore with hands that trembled in their impatience while their mouths clung in a moist frenzy of insatiable hunger.

'Ros,' he groaned, but his attempts to say more were stifled by the urgent ministrations of her mouth against his.

He tried to speak again, but again she prevented him. Then the movements of his hands against her body grew less random and more purposeful, as though urging a modicum of calm to the trembling urgency possessing her.

'There's no rush, darling,' he whispered huskily when at last she began heeding the message of those hands. 'We have all the time in the world.'

She shook her head as though to deny that claim, a nebulous fear of time—of time to think—creeping shadily into her consciousness. She wanted to be over-powered by passion, to take this one chance of giving total expression to the love within her. It was something she wanted above all else... but she wanted no time in which to contemplate the enormity of what she was committing herself to.

'Oh, but we have,' he insisted, easing her body a fraction from his, a luminous darkness in his eyes as his hands rose to the nape of her neck, only to slid slowly back downwards again.

An involuntary cry burst from her as shivers rippled down her spine in response to his touch and she was straining to move back to where she had been, her body craving the sensuous heat of his.

'No,' he whispered, holding her from him as his fingers seemed to tease against the catch of her bra.

When his hands this time made their journey up her body, it was in silky softness against her flesh, and they kept moving upwards and over her shoulders, then downwards—in one deft movement removing both her dress and her bra.

Her wide-eyed expression of total surprise brought laughter rumbling from him—yet still he resisted when she once again tried to fling herself back into his arms.

'No,' she choked, reaching out in an attempt to stop him as he sank to his knees before her, wanting only to feel him safely back in her arms.

'Yes,' he insisted, laughter still rumbling in him as his arms encircled her and he buried his face against the concave smoothness of her stomach.

Despite the sensuous slowness of his movements, she was left no time for the thoughts she so feared. She wound her fingers into his hair, gripping tightly, while the hot sweetness of his breath against her flesh sent fires searing through her and left her incapable of thought.

'Damian!' His name was an unspecified plea that was echoed in the tugging impatience of her hands in his hair.

'I've told you, darling, we have all the time in the world,' he breathed against her, while his fingers—with an ease that might have shocked her, had she been capable of registering further shock—freed her stockings and began sliding them one by one down her legs, his hands sensuously adhering to the shapely contours of each as they descended.

It was because she felt something was about to explode within her that she was forced to concentrate her mind on what was happening to her... And what was happening was that she was automatically obeying the instructions to step out of this and then that of a man who was slowly, and with graceful expertise, stripping every shred of clothing from her body!

It was in that moment when all the barriers she had erected against facing what she had committed herself to had tumbled from her mind that he lifted his head, his mouth curving in a quizzical smile as he gazed up at her. Her thoughts became scattered by the explosive force of the love that that smile kindled in her.

'So tell me, now that you've got me on my knees before you—in what you no doubt consider to be my rightful place—what do you intend doing with me?'

She intended loving him, she cried out silently, her hands moving to cup the sides of his head. The Sheridan blood in her would allow her but a single love in her lifetime—of that she had no doubt—and whatever moments she could steal of that love she would do so in full consciousness of what she was doing... and those memories would remain locked away in her heart until the day came when time had dulled her pain sufficiently for her to be able to resurrect them.

'I don't know about rightful place,' she whispered, the desolate ache of sadness catching in her words while her hands urged him up, 'but it definitely suits you.'

'If it suits me so, why are you hauling me to my feet?' he demanded huskily, rising. He cupped her face in his hands, the questioning in his eyes warning her that he had heard past her joking words to their underlying sadness. 'Ros?'

Still cupping his head in her hands, she drew it down to hers and kissed his lips, rejoicing as she felt the trembling urgency in her own body echo shudderingly in his.

'You're so beautiful,' he whispered hoarsely, drawing back from her, his eyes remaining locked with hers as his hands began tracing the curves of her body.

She hesitated only for the merest fraction of a second before slipping her own hands beneath the heavy silk of his dressing-gown and then sliding it down over his shoulders.

'How about undoing the belt first?' he teased softly, making no attempt to assist her.

She undid the belt, the breath catching in her throat as he shrugged free of the robe and stood in naked perfection before her.

'And you're beautiful,' she whispered, too enchanted by his beauty to care what his reaction might be to her use of such a word.

'Really?' he chuckled, apparently not in the least put out. 'But I'm afraid I wasn't nearly as much fun as you were to undress.'

She wondered at the composure in him that made it possible for him to laugh with such carefree softness at such a moment, then she found herself gazing deep into his eyes as he suddenly lifted her in his arms and carried her to the bed, and saw nothing even remotely resembling composure in them.

'You're shivering,' he whispered, wrapping his arms around her as he lay down beside her.

She wanted to point out that he was too, but his arms had tightened, drawing her body fiercely against the turgid heat of his, and the words were lost in the searing flame of need flaring between them.

She clung to him, the savage power of his arousal awakening not fear in her, but a restless impatience that his body, instead of answering the blindly uninhibited urgings of hers, was torturing her with its inexplicable restraint. But her impatience turned to soft, insuppressible moans of pleasure when his hands slowly swept her body, then to sharp cries when he lowered his head to her aching breasts and teased his lips against one desire-tautened nipple.

'Damian!' she cried out at a point when she felt she must explode, raking her nails mindlessly against his back, then pummelling him almost in anger when he lifted his head and gave a soft chuckle of triumph.

'I had to make sure you weren't about to change your mind,' he teased breathlessly, his body suddenly tensing.

'Are you completely mad?' croaked Rosanne, the accusation bursting out of her in an anguished plea.

'Completely,' he groaned, biting in passion against her bottom lip as he strove to still and prepare her.

He cried out her name as his body invaded hers in one searing moment of pain and pleasure. It was from the pain that she shrank only momentarily, but it was with a sob of pure joy that she welcomed the pleasure. Yet it was in those first moments of her total acceptance of him that she felt him resist—stilling her with the sheer force of his body as he whispered in ragged protest against her mouth.

'Tell me I'm only imagining this is your first time,' he pleaded.

She pressed her mouth against his in seductive impatience.

'Tell me!' he groaned.

'Damian, do we really have to discuss it right at this very moment?' she protested frantically.

'Ros, I...' His words petered away to a shuddered groan as his resistance finally gave way.

It was then that his body took command, its forceful exuberance triggering off a reaction in hers that sent devastating explosions blasting through her from head to toe. She bit against his shoulder as she tried to call his name and nothing came, then, as the breath trapped in her lungs burst from her, she felt that same devastating experience start to happen all over again.

There was a part of her that half wished for time to become suspended, just long enough for her to discover if this miracle was one they were both sharing. But it was her own body that finally gave her the answer; now attuning itself to his as though they had been locked in love for eternity, it instantly sensed the moment that miracle was about to be shared. And it was as her body became racked by the sweet, hot explosions shuddering through his that love and pleasure erupted within her with a force that she felt must tear her apart.

It was a long while before either of them had any breath to speak; they simply lay panting and spent in one another's arms, their bodies still locked in love.

'If I should die within the next few minutes,' were Damian's first, raggedly distorted words, 'which well I might, tell Bridie she's welcome to my body for her compost heap.'

It was several seconds later that Rosanne's starved lungs felt sufficiently replenished to attempt a reply.

'What?' she managed eloquently.

'And another thing,' continued Damian, easing his body from hers, but keeping her clasped firmly in his arms, 'have you been innoculated against rabies?'

'What?' If she was lucky, she told herself with a dreamy lack of concern, he would ask another question and she could trot out that same word for a third time from this rapturous cloud on which she was floating.

'If I didn't have this macho image to preserve, I might think about muzzling you the next time we make love.'

'The next time,' she sighed ecstatically. 'Damian, could the next time ever be as fantastic as——?' She broke off, crashing off her cloud with a thud as she realised what she was saying.

'Don't you dare start getting coy with me,' he growled lazily, rising on an elbow and gazing down at her from heavy-lidded, wickedly twinkling eyes. 'Fantastic's as good a word as any—until I come up with a more fitting superlative.'

'Do you really mean that?' she breathed, almost squirming with delight—she had no doubt whatever that he did.

'No—I was just being polite,' he chuckled, reaching out a finger and tracing it gently against her lower lip. 'Seems I inflicted a mite of damage on you too.'

'What do you mean?' she demanded contentedly, then her eyes widened in horror at the sight of what could only be her own teeth marks on his shoulder. 'Oh, no! Damian, is that what your remark about rabies was about?' she gasped in horror. 'I feel terrible! I didn't mean to hurt you! I——'

'Hey!' he interrupted with a chuckle, lowering his head and rubbing his nose teasingly against hers. 'Did I hurt you when I took that chunk out of your lip?'

'A chunk?' she gasped, her fingers flying to her mouth and finding it exceedingly tender as they explored it.

'Perhaps a chunk was a slight exaggeration,' he conceded, then he frowned, all trace of laughter leaving his face. 'But I did hurt you—right at the start.'

She shook her head, her eyes lowering from his.

'Ros, I've already warned you about going coy on me,' he reminded her sharply.

'Does it really matter?' she asked, feeling suddenly peculiarly threatened, yet puzzled as to why she should.

'Yes,' he replied uncooperatively. 'Ros, you're a woman of twenty-five!'

'What's my age got to do with it, for heaven's sake?' she protested, having only just bit back a correction in the nick of time.

'Ros, you know damned well what I'm getting at,' he sighed. 'You're an exceptionally beautiful and sexy woman—at least you are when you're not putting on that ice-maiden act you're so irritatingly partial to... So, why?'

'Why what?' she hedged, feeling more and more vulnerable and threatened with every passing moment and still having no idea why she should be.

With an exclamation of exasperation he flung himself flat on his back. 'I'm having considerable difficulty believing we're having this ridiculous conversation!'

'You're the one who started it,' she accused, while at the same time wanting to fling herself on him and bury herself in his arms.

'Hell, Ros, I've already admitted I can make neither head nor tail of you most of the time... but the last thing I ever imagined was that you'd be a virgin!'

'Why shouldn't I be?' she demanded, hurt to the quick. 'You make it sound as though I'm some sort of a freak!'

'God, I hope not!' he groaned, reaching out and drawing her against him. 'Ros, that's the last thing I intended to do. It's just that I'm not blind to the fact that you must have had men swarming around you in their droves, to put it mildly. So it must have been a conscious decision on your part not to become sexually involved with any of them—am I right?'

She gave a non-committal twitch, pressing her cheek against the warmth of his shoulder. She felt inexplicably secure now that his arms were around her once more—but it was an ephemeral security, too fragile for her to be able to point out that the missing ingredient in her previous relationships with men had been love.

'The logical conclusion would be that this would be something you'd only share with a man you loved—but that certainly counts me out.'

Rosanne was glad that she couldn't see his face—nor he hers, for that matter. Of course he would reach any logical conclusion there was to be reached—and that was what she had felt threatening her. But it threw her that he should have rejected the blatantly obvious with such utter certainty.

'What makes you so certain I'm not in love with you?' she asked guardedly and immediately wished she had phrased it in a way that sounded less of a challenge.

'Simple,' he chuckled, his arm tightening around her as he tucked her even closer to him. 'One of the things I've noticed about women who fancy themselves to be in love is the compulsion they seem to feel to share every detail of their life histories with the man concerned— and to dig out any detail they can of his. Whereas trying to get even the slightest scrap of information out of you is about as easy as extracting teeth.'

She laughed, but she might just as well have burst into tears, the way those words affected her. She stretched her arm across his darkly matted chest, deriving what little comfort she could from simply being able to do so.

'Have you ever been in love, Damian?' she asked, trying to hold the terrible desolation within her at bay by prolonging this illusory moment of peace.

'I've been fairly close to it . . . I think,' he murmured uncertainly, his fingers stroking absent-mindedly in her hair. 'Perhaps I'm the exception to the rule about Sheridans and their single block-buster of a love. Or perhaps——' He broke off with a lazy chuckle. 'This is beginning to get rather boringly introspective.'

'No, it's not,' she protested. She didn't care that she was being utterly irrational in wanting to prolong these precious moments for as long as she possibly could— she had never in her entire life felt as intensely happy and complete as she did now and, no matter what the future held, she would always have this memory. 'Or perhaps what?' she urged, sinking her fingers into his chest hairs and tugging gently.

'Or perhaps I've always backed away from relationships because of that wretched old wives' tale about the Sheridans,' he sighed. 'I've been hearing it since I was a kid and, to be frank, I've never seen it in the romantic light most seem to—in fact, it's always scared the hell out of me.'

Rosanne wanted to make a joking remark, but couldn't. She understood his feeling only too well. But he was wasting his time trying avoiding tactics, she thought sadly. Once his time had come, that love would sneak up on him and fell him whether he welcomed it or not—just as it had her.

'Poor Damian,' she whispered softly, but pain shivered through her at the knowledge of the passionate intensity that she knew he would one day give to loving someone other than herself, and decided that the words 'poor Rosanne' would have been far more appropriate.

'Let me tell you that "poor Damian" considers himself the most privileged of men—and the most contented,' he teased, turning and sliding down beside her until his face was level with hers. 'But why am I that man privileged above all others?' he asked huskily.

She lifted her head and pressed it against his cheek so that she wouldn't have to look into his eyes as she lied.

'Some strange sort of physical chemistry, I suppose.'

Already she could feel the wall of illusion with which she had so strenuously surrounded herself begin to crumble.

'Some strange sort of chemistry, indeed?' he teased, then added in a completely different tone, 'And you, Ros, have you ever been in love?'

She tried to shake her head, but even that unspoken lie refused to come.

'Have you?' he repeated.

'Yes.'

'The sort that scares the hell out of this coward?' he probed with a perception that disturbed her deeply.

She nodded.

'And I'm trespassing like an insensitive oaf with all these questions!' he exclaimed almost angrily. 'Ros, darling, forgive me!'

'How can I, when there's nothing to forgive?' she whispered, a sharp pang of guilt accompanying the love welling in her at his obvious concern.

'But I——'

'And you're not the only one never led where he doesn't wish to go,' she chided softly.

'That's not what I meant,' he sighed, then gave a lazy chuckle that shivered sensuously across her skin before adding, 'Though I'm most happy and relieved not to have a single doubt as to the validity of that particular claim of yours.'

She experienced another uneasy pang as she wondered how many of her claims he actually did doubt, but then his mouth and his hands swept all such thoughts from her mind as they began laying their magic siege to her instantly receptive body.

'It's beginning to appear that, whatever I suggest, you're going to disagree with it automatically,' stated Damian in ominously quiet tones as he scowled across the breakfast table at her.

Rosanne gazed down sightlessly at the plate before her. She had known that her moments of fairy-tale dreaming would be short-lived—but not as short as this, she thought numbly. She had floated into this day on a cloud of enchantment, her mind and body filled with bewitching secrets that only the man seated opposite her could share. And there *had* been that special sense of shared secrets between them, she reminded herself, desperation welling up within her as she sought futile comfort in the memories of only minutes before. She hadn't imagined that secret, sultry look that had been for her and her alone when Bridie had greeted the pair of them with martyred grumblings over the lateness of the hour that she was being required to serve breakfast. Damian's reply to his housekeeper's complaints had been a nonchalant grin, but it had been that sultry look of complicity they had shared before it, rather than any guilt, that had brought the rosy glow of consternation to her own cheeks.

Yet only moments later her world had begun disintegrating around her... a world she had created in her own mind out of her own romantic delusions.

'Why shouldn't I start trying to track down Hester's grandchild?' he challenged aggressively. 'The only way I'd feel safe about telling Hester would be if I found the girl, explained everything to her and was able to take her to Hester.'

'Damian, it could take forever, finding her,' protested Rosanne, still driven to fight on despite recognising the futility of her attempts to postpone the inevitable.

'Not with all the resources I can call on,' he informed her. 'I'll get someone investigating the nursing-home records right away and——'

'Damian——'

'What?' he almost spat at her. 'I'm wasting my time? It won't work? You can trot out all the negatives you like, but I'm not interested!' He slammed his knife and fork down on his plate, then pushed it aside. 'I was fool enough to allow last night to lull me into expecting what would amount to a miracle! I'll never be able to make you out, will I, Ros? Because that's the way you want it.' He moved his chair back from the table, as though trying to distance himself further from her. 'But the one thing I really can't understand is that you appear to be as ignorant about what makes me tick as I am about you—and one thing I'm not is secretive; I'm virtually an open book for anyone who cares to read me.'

'Damian . . . I didn't mean to upset you like——'

'Upset me?' he cut in coldly. 'Upset isn't quite the word I'd use—though God only knows what is! I say I don't think Hester should be told about her grand-child—Ros says she should. I say I'm going to try to trace the girl—and what does Ros immediately say?' He gave a grim laugh as he rose, flinging his napkin on the table. He gazed down at it for a moment, then picked it up and tossed it into the middle of the table. 'I'd say that napkin was white—what colour would you say it was, darling?'

Rosanne folded her own napkin and placed it on the table, her world disintegrating around her.

'I'll get on with working on the diaries,' she told him in a voice that astounded her with its calm control. 'The sooner I finish them, the sooner I can leave.'

Less than half an hour ago she had still been so ab-sorbed by her own self-delusions that she had managed to blot out all concept of reality . . . And now she was bracing herself against the devastating onslaught of re-ality as she heard Damian's footsteps approach her side of the table.

'Why this sudden rush to leave, Ros?' he asked, his tone no more than faintly enquiring as he drew to a halt behind her chair.

'I . . . I just feel it would be better if I left as soon as possible,' she stammered hoarsely, her eyes trained on her hands, which were clenched and white-knuckled on her lap.

'Dear me,' he drawled in mock surprise. 'You're not by any chance telling me I'm being relegated to no more than a one-night stand, are you?'

'Damian, please,' she begged, a trembling limpness sliding into her and filling the spaces left by the strength ebbing inexorably from her.

'Darling, you don't seem to realise——'

'Don't!' she choked, the word deteriorating into a sob as everything within her seemed to crumble and collapse.

'Ros, what is it?' he exclaimed, dragging her chair round and squatting down beside her. 'You can't believe I was serious when I made that snide one-night stand remark!'

'I didn't,' she sobbed. 'Damian, I——'

'Darling, don't cry,' he begged. 'Please, don't cry!' With a muttered oath, he pulled her into his arms, hugging her tightly to him as he raised them both to their feet.

'The things I've done!' she sobbed incoherently. 'You'll never understand——'

'Damian!' Bridie burst into the room, her expression distraught. 'It's Rosanne Fogarty on the phone. Hester's taken a turn for the worse and she's in hospital!'

CHAPTER NINE

'SEE if you can persuade him to let you drive part of the way,' Bridie had advised as she and James had fussed and fretted around both Rosanne and Damian before they had left on their journey south. 'Though God only knows if you'll be in any fit state to offer once you've had a taste of Damian's driving—especially in that fancy Italian car he'll no doubt be taking. They shouldn't allow contraptions like that on to the roads—they go far too fast!'

A faint smile hovered on Rosanne's lips as she remembered those words, and James's solemn-faced nods of agreement with his wife's every word. She glanced briefly through the window, wincing as she quickly averted her eyes from it. No doubt they had passed through some magnificent countryside during the past couple of hours, she told herself resignedly, but at a speed that had, for the best part of that time, reduced it to no more than an alarming blur.

'If you'd like me to drive, I'd be quite happy to,' she offered, virtually certain that he would refuse.

'I suppose that was another of James's or Bridie's bright suggestions,' muttered Damian, in almost the first full sentence he had uttered since they had begun their journey.

'Damian, they were only thinking of you and they were right to suggest someone come with you.' And because nothing on earth would have stopped her coming with him she was profoundly grateful to Bridie and James for their voluble insistence that someone, preferably she, should accompany him. 'You shouldn't be alone at a time like this,' she added quietly, and then, with a fatalistic acceptance that soon she would never again have an opportunity to do so, she leaned towards him and pressed her cheek briefly against his shoulder in a silent gesture of love.

'What was that all about?' he asked brusquely, his eyes never once straying from the road ahead.

'It was——' She broke off with a sigh of frustration, furious with herself for her stupidity in leaving herself open to such pointed rejection. 'I suppose I was attempting to show a little sympathy,' she muttered resignedly.

'I see. A tactile variation of, "There, there, sonny—everything will be all right."'

Those cold, drawling words were like a slap in the face.

'Damian, I know how worried you must be about Hester,' she said, battling to keep calm, 'but behaving like this won't help.'

'I'm not the one who insisted on your tagging along with me,' he retorted coldly. 'So I'm afraid you'll just have to take me as you find me. But what really puzzles me—and, as you know, just about everything about you puzzles me—is your amazing backing of Bridie's contention that I shouldn't be let loose on my own. After all, not that long before, you'd been hell-bent on getting away from me altogether.'

Rosanne glanced sharply at his grim profile, the unmistakable bitterness in his words starting up a strange, fluttering ache in the pit of her stomach.

For a fraction of a second he turned, his eyes cold and implacable as they met hers. 'Well, it's true, isn't it?'

Whatever the feeling had been, it died in her at the sight of his eyes. The only hurt she had inflicted on him, she told herself bitterly, was in an area where just about any woman could hurt any man—his masculine pride.

'I'm worried about Hester too—if it's of any interest to you,' she muttered dejectedly, the feeling of sick dread that she had so long been trying to hold at bay filling her as she uttered her grandmother's name.

'It is,' he conceded, then added accusingly, 'Though that's just about the only thing we appear to have in common.'

It wasn't until they reached the outskirts of Dublin that he spoke again.

'I've a small place off the Balls Bridge Road,' he suddenly announced. 'We'll use that rather than put Hank and Rosanne to any trouble.'

Rosanne felt a momentary pang of relief, then gave a mental shrug: the possibility of coming face to face with her namesake was the least of her problems.

'In fact,' Damian continued, 'I think the best thing would be for me to drop you off at the flat. I want to call in on Rosanne and Hank before going to the hospital.'

The rain, which had fallen intermittently on their journey south, was tumbling heavily from blackened skies by the time they turned up the drive to an opulently modern block of flats set back from the road in lushly wooded surroundings. It was still only early afternoon, but it might as well have been late night, given the stormy darkness of the skies and the extravagant blaze of lights coming from the building.

Rosanne started in surprise as a uniformed doorman appeared and helped her out of the car, protecting her with a voluminous black umbrella. Shivering in the cold, she waited at the top of the marbled steps leading into a foyer that many a luxury hotel might have envied— watching as the heavily braided doorman returned to Damian.

'It's good to see you, Kevin,' Damian greeted him, unlocking the boot of the car.

'Your housekeeper rang and the place has been prepared for you,' the doorman told him, helping him remove the luggage from the car. 'I was very sorry to hear about Miss Hester—have you had any more news on how she is?'

Damian shook his head as the two men mounted the steps towards Rosanne. 'But I'll be going along to the hospital just now,' he said, then hesitated, glancing briefly at Rosanne before turning back to the doorman. 'I have to go round to the Fogartys' first—where Hester's been staying. Perhaps you wouldn't mind getting the young lady settled in while I do that?'

The doorman clapped him firmly on the shoulder. 'You be on your way. And don't you worry about the wee girl; I'll see she's settled in all right.'

Telling herself she was being petty and unreasonable, Rosanne tried to push aside all thoughts about the fact that, not only had he not even said a word of goodbye to her, but Damian hadn't even looked in her direction before returning to the car and driving off. But her head was swimming with the effort by the time she entered the lift with the doorman, and she found it impossible to shake off a ludicrous feeling of having been completely abandoned.

'What did you say your name was?' asked the doorman, his tone friendly and solicitous.

'Ros—Ros Grant.'

'Ros—now that's a lovely name,' he stated with that curious blend of courtesy and familiarity she had met so often and found so appealing in Ireland. 'But I'm afraid it's sad times that have brought you here,' he added with a sigh.

Rosanne nodded, touched by his obviously genuine concern, then stepped out of the lift on to what appeared to be a mezzanine floor. She followed her companion up a short flight of stairs and then through the entrance door he unlocked.

She stepped inside and gazed round her in complete disbelief. A greater contrast to the gracious, old-world elegance of Sheridan Hall, she couldn't imagine. The penthouse flat in which she now found herself had no shortage of gracious elegance, but it was of the minimal, starkly restrained type that spoke of very modern and ruinously expensive interior designers.

'Why don't you make yourself a cup of tea and have a nice relax?' called Kevin as he disappeared with the luggage. 'There's everything in the kitchen.'

'I think I'll do that,' said Rosanne faintly when he reappeared moments later—still completely awed by the delicate lavishness of her cream-on-cream surroundings.

'Are you sure you'll be all right, now?'

'I'll be fine,' she smiled. 'And thank you very much for all your help.'

'Sure it was nothing,' he protested. 'And if you need me for anything, just dial nine on your telephone—oh, and you'll be needing these.'

He pressed keys into her hand and left.

The instant he had gone she found herself wondering if she should have tipped him. Then it was pondering over the problem as to whether or not he might have been insulted had she that kept her mind occupied for the next several moments.

In the end she sat wearily on the edge of the nearest of the pale cream leather armchairs and began asking herself just how much longer she would be able to go on occupying her mind with nothing but trivia... It was time she dragged her head from the sand and faced reality head-on.

But deciding she must face up to reality and actually doing so were two very different matters, she discovered

when she had showered, changed into a comfortable
housecoat and taken herself off on a half-hearted potter
around the apartment, all the while waiting for her
thoughts to co-operate. It was as though, ever since she
had arrived in Ireland, her mind had decided that the
only way it could cope was by rigid compartmentalis-
ation of her problems, ruthlessly isolating each from the
next lest the whole be too terrible for her to contemplate . . . till she had reached this ghastly state where she
was practically incapable of rational thought, she pointed
out to herself miserably.

She moved listlessly towards the huge plate-glass
window comprising the outer walls of the living area,
parting the silken cream of the ceiling-to-floor swath of
curtains to gaze down on the city twinkling brightly
below. It was the city to which her grandmother had
come to say her final farewells, she thought with an
aching sadness. And it was the city in which grandmother and granddaughter would at last be united, she
vowed fiercely.

Hester, she knew, would understand and forgive the
terrible bitterness with which she, Rosanne, had originally come in search of her . . . just as she knew Damian
probably never would.

She left the window and sat down on one of the huge
cream leather sofas, frowning as she gazed around the
impersonal perfection surrounding her. Then she gave a
half-smile as Hester's chirpy voice seemed to dance in
her ears.

'It's too perfect, isn't it, my dear? It lacks the clutter
of soul.'

And that was exactly what Hester would say—
probably had said—Rosanne realised bemusedly as she
slipped off her shoes and lay down, her mind suddenly
crystal-clear.

Whether or not Damian would ever forgive her for the underhand way she had sought out her grandmother was completely immaterial, she accepted, her eyes closing, because he would certainly never forgive her for what she was about to do—what she felt it her duty, both to herself and to Hester, to do as soon as she possibly could.

'Ros—wake up! I'm sorry I was gone so long.'

Rosanne woke with a start, her eyes wide with bewilderment as she struggled to get her bearings.

'I'm sorry, I must have . . . oh, my God, Hester—how is she?' she burst out anxiously, suddenly wide awake.

'Not as bad as I'd managed to work myself up into expecting her to be,' said Damian, his eyes blank with weariness as he sat down on the sofa beside her, rain glistening in his hair and on the shoulders of his overcoat. 'She's very weak, but . . .'

Rosanne struggled to her knees in consternation beside him as his voice broke.

'But she's still very much the same Hester,' he finished raggedly.

'Damian, let me take your coat,' she offered, and began gently pulling it down over his unresisting shoulders when he made no reply.

His movements almost dazed, he rose to his feet when she urged him to, but made no effort to assist her when she too rose and finished removing his coat from him.

'You're soaking!' she exclaimed anxiously. 'Why don't you have a shower, or a bath, while I make some tea?'

The look with which he responded to her words was completely blank.

'You've had a very long day of it,' she remarked softly, catching him by the arm and, when he still failed to react, steering him towards one of the two large bedrooms, each with its palatial adjoining bathroom. 'There are a few cold things in the fridge—would you like me to make you a sandwich?'

He shook his head.

'Right—I'll make that tea . . . while you shower,' she added, almost as she might have to a child she was trying to coax into action, when he showed no sign of moving from where he stood in the middle of the darkly marbled bathroom floor.

Her face was drawn with worry as she made her way to the kitchen and put on the kettle. Short of stripping him and forcibly bathing him, there was little else she could have done, she told herself fretfully, then gave a groan of utter hopelessness. She didn't need this, she told herself wearily: tonight, for the first time since she had arrived in Ireland, she had managed to get things sorted out in her mind . . . and she knew that the decisions she had come to were the right ones. And nothing was going to make her change her mind now—no matter what it cost her!

She finished making the tea and placed a cover on the teapot then, with visions of Damian still standing where she had left him, returned to the bathroom and knocked on the door. She was just about to knock a second time when the door opened.

'Yes?' he asked, his hair and body glistening wet as he fastened a towel round his waist.

'I just thought I'd let you know the tea was made,' she said, the searing vividness of the memories hotly flooding her almost overwhelming her as she caught sight of the small area of bruising that her own passionate abandonment had so recently inflicted on his shoulder.

'Thanks,' he replied, turning from the door. 'I shan't be long.'

And in that moment it would have taken very little to convince her that she had imagined every second of every hour of that night shared in passion.

When he joined her in the living-room he had put on a soft white towelling robe, but he had obviously made no attempt to dry the hair that still dripped in rivulets down his face.

After a few sips of her own tea, she found that she couldn't stand watching the water dripping intermittently from his hair to his cup as he unconcernedly drank from it.

She went to the bathroom and returned with a hand-towel, and it was only when she removed the cup from his unresisting hand that his face registered anything—and then it was only faint bemusement. She returned his cup to its saucer on the table, then climbed on to the sofa and knelt beside him.

'Right—let's do something about drying your hair,' she stated, placing the towel over his head.

'I'm perfectly capable of drying my own hair,' he muttered, but he made no move to free himself of the towel.

'Well, why didn't you do so?' she retorted and began vigorously towelling dry his hair.

For a moment he sat absolutely stock still, then his shoulders sagged and his head fell forward against her, almost toppling her over.

'If you don't mind, I'd rather be alone.'

His words, muffled against her, had thrown her, but it was the sudden, jarring heave of his shoulders that cut through her puzzlement, affecting her own body as though it were an extension of his. She removed the towel from his head and dropped it on the floor, then wrapped her arms tightly around him. Still holding him to her, she extricated her legs from beneath her and lay back, drawing him with her till he lay with his head cradled against her.

The dampness from his hair was cold as it permeated the material of her housecoat, but his tears were like a scalding heat.

'If only there was the time!' he protested in anger and hopelessness. 'Just the time to find her granddaughter and bring them together. I know the pleasure it would bring her would far outweigh any pain!'

His tormented words cut through Rosanne like a jabbing knife. She hugged him to her, frantically telling herself that, no matter how unbearable she found his pain, she mustn't even consider telling him the truth. Nothing could rid her of the nagging certainty that if she did he would rather kill her than allow her to see her grandmother.

'Damian, perhaps there will be the time,' she soothed helplessly, loathing herself for such duplicity, yet unable to think of any other words that might offer comfort.

'There won't be,' he raged against her. 'The doctors made that plain.'

There were tears misting her eyes as she laid her cheek against his damp head.

'My poor Damian,' she whispered sadly, rocking him gently to her.

'No!' he groaned, tearing himself free with a muttered oath, then sitting upright. Without another word he retrieved the towel from the floor and began rubbing it angrily against his hair.

'Damian, I . . . I——'

'You what?' he snapped aggressively.

Stunned and hurt, she rounded on him. 'That's right—take it out on me!' she exploded. 'Just because you're embarrassed by tears anyone else would consider perfectly human——'

'If you think I'm embarrassed by a few tears, you know me even less than I'd suspected.' He flung the towel down in a gesture of angry frustration. 'What the hell am I saying?' he groaned. 'You know me as well as I know you—which, in plain English, means you don't know me at all!'

'How can you say that?' she blurted out, hurt choking her words.

'How can I say it?' he asked with a harsh laugh, leaning back against the sofa and gazing up at the ceiling. 'Perhaps because, if I am going to blub like a baby for the first time in God knows how many years, I'd rather do it alone—or at least not in the presence of someone so busy keeping me at such a mental arm's length that I scarcely know her any better now than I did the day I first clapped eyes on her!'

'Is that what I was to you last night?' she choked, unable to stop herself. 'A virtual stranger...keeping you at arm's length?'

She sensed the increase in tension in him as her words hit home.

'Ros, I'm tired and sorely troubled right now,' he muttered tonelessly. 'This isn't the time to be having a conversation like this.'

'The point is that we *are* having it,' she persisted, something over which she had no control driving her, 'so perhaps you'd be good enough to answer my question.'

'OK,' he sighed. 'The answer is yes. If you recall, I said that you kept me at a *mental* arm's length and, quite frankly, there have been the odd occasions when I've found myself physically attracted to a beautiful stranger... and, I'm sure, had I taken any one of them into my bed for the night, I'd have known a darned sight more about them than I did you, come the morning.'

With his words reverberating in her ears, Rosanne dragged herself to her feet, her only aim to get out of the room and out of his sight before she disintegrated completely.

'Look, Ros, I——'

'Damian, whatever you do, don't apologise,' she interrupted in tones she found astoundingly controlled. 'I asked you a question and you gave me a truthful answer. I...it's rather late...I think I'll turn in now.' Even as she was uttering those disjointed words she had already begun to break up inside and it was all she could do to stop herself from breaking into a run as she left and made her way to her bedroom.

She closed the door behind her and, still holding herself back from running, she walked in darkness to the huge window comprising almost a total wall of the room and rested her burning forehead against the sharp coldness of the glass.

For several seconds she stood there, the only sound in the room the harsh rasp of the sobs choking from her as she battled to regain control of herself. As the sobs gradually subsided, she found herself gazing out through the blur of her tears on the city twinkling in merry indifference below. Somewhere in that vast sprawl was Hester, she told herself...her grandmother. What she called her was immaterial; somewhere out there was the grandmother she had begun to love, even while in her heart she had tried to hate her.

'Ros?'

She gave a start, angrily scrubbing at her tear-streaked cheeks. A second ago she had been so engrossed in her thoughts that she hadn't even heard the door open—now her every sense was in a turmoil of awareness of his presence.

'Yes, you did ask me a question,' he stated quietly as he joined her by the window. 'But the answer I gave you certainly wasn't honest.'

'It doesn't matter,' she replied wearily and, in her desperation to drop the subject, added, 'I was wondering where Hester was...among all those thousands of lights.'

She sensed rather than saw the sharp look of puzzlement he gave her before he leaned closer to the window and looked out at lights stretching for miles before them.

'If you look over there to the right,' he said eventually, 'there's a dark patch—can you see it?'

Her eyes followed where his hand pointed, then she nodded.

'The dark patch is the park beside the clinic and to the left of it, right in front of that tall, flashing beacon, is the clinic itself.'

She nodded again as she located the precise position and felt a strange easing of the terrible tension gripping her. It was fanciful in the extreme to think that knowing exactly where her grandmother was could possibly have any effect on her—but that was how it felt.

'Ros, you're wrong in what you said just now—it *does* matter,' he suddenly protested. 'If I'd been honest I'd have admitted that my pride simply isn't up to handling the fact that you could share what you did with me last night and yet…oh, hell, Ros!' he groaned, cutting short his words. 'He's not dead is he—this man you love?'

She spun round to face him, horror on her face as she realised the tortuous path along which her face-saving lie had led them both.

'No!' She shook her head in frantic denial.

'Well, he could have been, for all I know,' he sighed, his words tinged with relief. 'I suppose what I'm really finding so difficult to swallow is the fact that, had you had the choice, I'm not the man with whom you'd have spent last night.'

'Oh, Damian,' she whispered hopelessly, yet even as she was wondering where she could possibly go from there he had already turned away from her with a muttered apology.

He halted halfway across the room. 'And that's honestly why I came here—to apologise,' he sighed. 'But, as you're no doubt aware, tact has never been my strong point and I've probably only succeeded in making things worse.'

She gazed across the darkness at the shadowy outline of his tall figure, the love for him in her swelling so powerfully that she wondered at his not recoiling from its blast.

'You're not the most tactful man I've ever known,' she heard her own voice agreeing. 'But you're the only man I'd have chosen to spend last—or any other—night with.'

There was no point in trying to retract the words, she told herself with a fatalistic resignation as he began walking back towards her.

'Thanks for that valiant attempt to massage my irrationally wounded pride,' he murmured, while giving her a mocking bow. 'And now I'll bid you goodnight.'

'Your pride wouldn't need any massaging,' she said, caught completely off guard by his cynical dismissal, 'if only you had the sense to believe what I said.'

And now she really had said far, far too much, she warned herself as she tried to ward off the feelings of reckless desperation spreading through her at the thought of how little time she had left.

'Why should I believe you,' he demanded harshly, 'when half the time you might just as well be speaking a foreign language for all the sense you make?' He dragged a hand exasperatedly through his hair. 'Whatever your game is, Ros, I've far too much on my plate right now even to be tempted to join in.'

'Damian, I'm sorry—I...' Her words choked to a halt in her throat.

Frowning, he took a step nearer her, then took her by the chin and tilted her face upwards.

'You're crying!' he exclaimed, his words part accusing, part uncertain.

'So were you earlier,' she choked irrationally, twisting free her face.

He gave a soft groan of exasperation as his hands descended on her shoulders.

'And earlier you comforted me,' he sighed. 'But the trouble is that if I take you in my arms it won't be to say, "There, there."'

'I don't want you to say, "There, there"!' she exploded, her new-found sense of reality deserting her as she flung herself against him, willing him to take her in his arms and still time forever.

She stirred to the sensation of fingers lazily tracing the outline of her mouth, a sensuous ache throbbing through her body as it too stirred in immediate response. Then her eyes opened and found themselves almost level with the enigmatic blue gaze of those of the man squatting at the side of the bed—the man whose turbulent passion had made time stand still for them both during those love-filled hours of the night.

'No—don't get up,' he whispered, his hand reaching out to press her back against the pillows as she made to sit up.

'But you're dressed!' Her husky words of accusation were an artless betrayal of the constancy of the need within her.

'Too right I'm dressed,' he teased, the softness of his accompanying laughter music to her ears. 'Right down to my overcoat.'

Her eyes, having ascertained the truth of that statement, widened in spontaneous consternation.

'I've also been creeping around the place like a thief for fear of wakening you,' he added with a lazy grin.

'Why?' she protested, reaching out and winding her arms tightly around his neck.

'For precisely this reason,' he groaned exasperatedly, his head, as though against his will, lowering to hers. 'I knew only too well how disastrously depleted my resistance would be,' he sighed, his words a warm breath against her parted mouth before his own crushed down on it.

As his lips renewed their endless search against hers, she was securely back in that illusory world of her own creation, to which reality could never gain entrance.

'Darling, no!' he protested in a distorted voice as he drew back from her. He cleared his throat as he gazed pleadingly at her. 'I've made you some tea,' he whispered, then gave a wry smile at the incongruity of his words.

Her eyes following his, she saw the mug of tea standing on the bedside table.

'How very kind of you,' she murmured uncertainly—all she wanted was to be back in the oblivion of his arms. 'Damian——'

'No! Ros, I have to go!' he exclaimed, tearing himself from her and straightening. 'Darling, I'm sorry,' he whispered, his expression a mixture of exasperation and regret as he gazed down at her.

And suddenly her mind was cleared of the blissful fog of delusion clouding it. She felt the cold chill of desolation rampage through her, ruthlessly laying waste the last vestiges of the magic to which she had so desperately clung. She sat up, hugging the bedclothes around her naked body as her mind formed the words that she knew she must say.

'I want to see Hester.' She had even made them sound like the death-knell they were, she accused herself bitterly, while a charged silence seemed to fill the room.

Her eyes rose to his and she hugged the bedclothes even tighter around her, as though trying to compensate for the icy blankness they encountered.

'I'm afraid that won't be possible,' he stated. 'At the moment the Fogartys and I are the only ones allowed to see her.'

Whether he was lying or not was immaterial, she told herself fatalistically, because the truth was that he didn't trust her—and how right he was not to.

'I understand,' she said quietly... She would simply have to find another way.

He glanced down at his watch, his body language loaded with tension and lack of ease.

'I must go,' he muttered uncomfortably. 'Hank's arranged for us to see a specialist friend of his at one of the other hospitals at nine-thirty—and I'd like to drop in on Hester first.'

He turned away from her and began walking towards the door, the spell between them gone as though it had never existed.

'Give Hester my love,' Rosanne called after him, picking up the mug of tea and pressing it to her lips to still their trembling.

He opened the door, then turned to face her, an almost haunted look momentarily chasing the anger from his expression.

'Off you go,' she urged, pressing the mug painfully against her bottom lip. 'You're not the only one around here with sorely depleted resistance.'

CHAPTER TEN

'SO—YOU told them you were my granddaughter, did you?' chuckled Hester.

It was all Rosanne could do not to wince as she rued not having had the presence of mind to claim any relationship other than that to the clinic authorities.

'I had a feeling it might be you, my dear child.'

Terrified that she was about to break down, Rosanne tried to get a grip on herself as she gazed down at the gaunt features of her grandmother. And it was partly to satisfy an overwhelming need in her and partly to hide the tears brimming in her eyes that she bent down and pressed her firm young cheek against a pallid old one.

'It's so good to see you,' she choked.

She felt Hester's hand pat soothingly against her hair.

'And it's good to see you, my darling—even though you are in a bit of a state,' murmured the old lady.

Rosanne's head jerked up, guilt and consternation in her face.

'But I'd say you've been having a pretty tough time of it, one way or another, ever since you joined us, haven't you, darling?' continued Hester gently. 'Though you could hardly expect falling in love with a man like my Damian to be easy—now could you?'

'No, I suppose I couldn't,' agreed Rosanne, smiling with resignation through her tears.

'I saw it coming from the start,' sighed Hester, then shook her head sadly. 'Believe me, I know what a terror he can be where women are concerned, but I've never seen him react to one as he did to you. You could have had him on a plate—yet now you seem to have blown your chance,' she stated with devastating candour. 'But one thing I find most puzzling is his not wanting you coming here to see me. He got very cagey and uncoop- erative when I suggested you get in by doing as you did— claiming to be a relative.' The faded blue eyes met Rosanne's in piercing question. 'Now that tells me there's far more to all this than I'll ever be able to puzzle out for myself...so I hope you're here to explain to me what it is.'

Rosanne took one frail hand and clasped it between both of hers.

'What I came here to tell you has nothing to do with Damian,' she said hoarsely.

'But, whatever it is, he's determined to protect me from it...and therefore from you?'

Rosanne nodded, wondering how she could possibly go on.

'Darling, I haven't much time left—but I'd like to see the pair of you properly sorted out before I go. And, whatever it is Damian feels I need protecting from, you obviously feel I don't.'

'I could be wrong...so terribly wrong!' choked Rosanne, her hands tightening compulsively on that of her grandmother. 'But I want you to know that I love you,' she said, her voice firming with resolution. 'That I would have loved you anyway—even though my name is Rosanne Bryant and I'm your granddaughter.'

For a moment there was an unbearable silence, then Rosanne leapt to her feet in terror at the terrible choking sound emanating from the old lady now lying in slumped pallor with her eyes tightly closed.

'I'll get a doctor!' she cried out in panic.

'No!' Hester shook her head vehemently.

'I shouldn't have broken it to you like that! I——'

'Just tell me, my darling child,' begged the old lady. 'For God's sake, *tell* me!'

As the words began tumbling from her, Rosanne sat on the bed and, placing an arm around her, cradled her grandmother to her. There were times when Hester sobbed like a child, berating herself for never having had the courage to read her husband's diaries. And there were times when they wept together, each in turn comforting the other.

'How could my boy possibly think something like this could be kept from me?' choked Hester, her words deteriorating into broken ramblings. 'Why didn't I have the strength of my convictions and contact Edward Bryant after George had died?' she raged. 'In offering Bryant's the biography, I felt I was offering an olive-branch! He knew then! How?'

'The woman who'd been matron at the nursing home where I was born contacted him after... after——'

'After George died!' exclaimed Hester bitterly. 'Why, oh why didn't I read those diaries? Why——?'

'It doesn't matter,' protested Rosanne tearfully. 'Nothing matters as long as we're together... as long as you can forgive me for the terrible way I sneaked into your life!'

'How can I blame you for having behaved as you did, knowing what you had little option but to believe of me then?' sighed Hester, her hand patting in understanding against Rosanne's.

'But I'm sure Grandpa Ted would find it hard to forgive me behaviour as low as that! He never judged you, he was too good and decent a person to——'

'Hush, my darling child—as you so rightly say, none of that matters any more.'

They talked on while time sped by unnoticed, cross-examining one another, sharing tears and, eventually, sharing the miracle of laughter.

'I can understand how you found it impossible to confide in Damian,' sighed Hester, her expression turning to one of brooding perplexity. 'But what are we to do about that now?'

'Nothing,' stated Rosanne bleakly. 'There's nothing that can be done. I always felt you would understand and forgive me—just as I've always felt Damian never would.'

'Darling, Damian's over-protectiveness of me verges on the unbalanced, I know that—but he's found it impossible to come to terms with the fact that I'm dying,' sighed Hester with devastating candour, while making no attempt to deny Rosanne's hopeless words. 'And unfortunately he had his suspicions of you right from the start—as he no doubt made you aware.'

'He told me he'd kill me if I hurt you.'

'Yes, that sounds like Damian at his subtle best,' murmured the old lady wryly. 'He's an enchanting, highly intelligent man, but beneath that charming surface lies a passionate and deeply complex nature. Losing the parents he adored—and, my God, how those two adored him in return—while he was still in his adolescent years might easily have destroyed a lesser character than Damian's. It was the same when he had to give up polo, which he'd lived for till then——'

She broke off, frowning as she became momentarily lost in her own private thoughts. 'Damian has what I can only describe as an almost infallible sixth sense, which he acts on almost as he breathes. You came up against it the moment you arrived, and it was that same sense, all those years ago when he lost his parents, that told him I needed him almost as much as he needed me. It was what coloured his attitude to George—and, dear God, how accurate it was in that respect.'

'And over me,' pointed out Rosanne numbly.

'Perhaps,' hedged Hester with a sigh. 'But do you really understand what it is you're up against with him, my darling?'

Rosanne nodded. She understood and had done so from the start. 'It's not simply all the deception and the fact I couldn't bring myself to tell him the truth even when we read the diaries together—though that's unforgivable enough. He will never forgive me for the harm I originally intended you; but, most of all, it's the terrible risk I've taken today in going against him and telling you the truth . . . for that he'll never forgive me.'

'Yet you tell me he wanted to search you out and bring you to me,' pointed out Hester gently, reaching up and stroking Rosanne's cheek in a gesture brimming over with love and understanding. 'But pointing out that to him isn't going to get us anywhere, as we both know. So I . . . Damian, darling! What a lovely surprise!'

Rosanne's reaction was one of fear: a debilitating, sickening fear that flooded through every part of her and which the reassuring squeeze of her grandmother's hand was powerless to lessen in any way.

'Ros, what are you doing here?' demanded Damian, striding over to the bed, a nurse in his wake. 'I told you——'

'Rosanne—sorry, I mean Ros—decided to visit me,' interrupted Hester. 'And I can't begin to tell you how happy I am she did.'

'I'm afraid it's strictly one visitor at a time, Mrs Cranleigh,' murmured the nurse apologetically, leaning over her. 'And we'll have to do something about getting this bed tidied up before Matron and your consultants arrive.'

Rosanne leapt to her feet in guilty confusion. For so long now she had lived with the horror of knowing that this moment would come, and now that it had her only thought was to avoid those steely blue eyes which she could, at that very instant, feel drilling into her.

'Off you go, darling,' murmured Hester, gazing encouragingly at her. 'But give me a kiss before you do.'

Rosanne bent down and kissed her grandmother, fighting against flinging her arms round her.

'I'll sort him out, don't you worry,' whispered Hester reassuringly in her ear.

'What makes you think I need any sorting out?' demanded Damian instantly, an edge of anger in his drawling tone.

As her grandmother embarked on a light-hearted reply, Rosanne fled to the door.

'And how do you plan getting back to the flat?' Damian called after her.

'I'll get a taxi,' she replied without turning.

'And I suggest you also see about getting yourself something to eat—I'm likely to be here for the rest of the day and well into the night.'

It was past midnight when he eventually returned.

In the first of those long, harrowing hours of her wait, Rosanne had twice picked up the telephone with the intention of booking herself into a hotel and leaving before he returned.

Later it was only the occasional longing look that she cast in the direction of the telephone, having accepted in her heart of hearts that she owed it both to herself and to him to face him. The past weeks of dishonesty and deception were a part of the nightmare she had to try to put behind her, and in order to do so she must stand up and face the truth, no matter what it cost her.

'What the hell are you doing here?' Damian flung at her savagely as she rose to her feet.

Rosanne's hand flew involuntarily to her mouth to stifle her horror. It wasn't just the bearded growth darkening his face that gave him a wild, almost ravaged appearance—it was what burned in his eyes with a glittering, terrible darkness.

'Hester!' she cried. 'Damian, is she——?'

'I asked you what the hell you were doing here,' he rasped, striding angrily up to her.

Rosanne took a terrified step back and fell awkwardly on to the sofa.

'I'm here only because I felt the time had come to face you rather than run,' she whispered raggedly. 'Damian, please—tell me that Hester's all right,' she pleaded.

'Why?' he snarled. 'So that you needn't feel guilty over what you've done?'

'Because I love her!' shrieked Rosanne, close to breaking-point. 'You said yourself the only way you could tell her was if you had me to take to her.'

'No—not you! You were not the granddaughter I had in mind when I said that!' he raged, hauling her to her feet and shaking her in fury. 'I wasn't thinking in terms of a vicious little viper who had already slunk into Hester's life with nothing but vengeance in her heart!' He flung her angrily from him, then began pacing up and down the room. 'To think I tried to tell myself I was crazy—that it was my imagination that you would sometimes look at her almost with hatred in your eyes!'

'I was wrong—terribly wrong,' she protested hoarsely. 'But I thought——'

'And now you're telling me you love her,' he cut through her protest with sneering disgust.

'I do! I'd started to love her even when I wanted to feel nothing but hatred for her. I'll never forgive myself for the way I've behaved.'

'Don't think you're the only one,' he snarled, again striding threateningly towards her. 'You knew she was a sick old woman even before you came to persecute her—you knew she was dying, for God's sake, and still you came! You came and you ferreted around in her life, looking for the best way to wreak your revenge on her, and you were prepared to let nothing stand in your way!'

'Damian, please!' she begged hoarsely. 'There's nothing you can say that I haven't already said to myself a thousand times over. But Hester has forgiven me...and surely even you can see that I did the right thing in telling her the truth. Of course she was devastated...but she was so happy too...she...' Her words deteriorated to a sob.

'You're right she was devastated,' he informed her, the sudden quietness of his tone filling her with far more fear than his previous rage. 'But you didn't see the true extent of that devastation—it began hitting her fully only a few hours ago and——' He stopped abruptly, turning and making his way to the window, his gait almost drunken.

With a howl of anguish, Rosanne raced to his side.

'Damian!' she pleaded, her hands tugging frantically at his arm.

'She slipped into a coma about an hour ago,' he stated tonelessly. 'The doctors can't say whether it was the shock or——' He broke off, grasping her fiercely by the shoulders. 'But I can say! I can most definitely say, can't I, Ros?' His fingers bit painfully into her flesh. 'Ros! How remiss of me—it's Rosanne. And let me see—it's twenty-four you are, not twenty-five. But how difficult it must have made life for you—my not being the complete walk-over Hester was.' The laugh he gave was chilling in its total lack of humour. 'And poor Hester, God love her, also suffers from the delusion that you love me. Whereas you and I know it's some other poor devil who has that honour. Did you hope to undo some of the harm you'd already done by stringing her along with that lie—or what?'

'I didn't lie to her,' stated Rosanne from between shock-frozen lips. And now the time for lies—all lies—was over. 'It's just that I happened to make an already complicated situation that much worse for myself by falling in love with you—that's what!'

His hands dropped from her as though they had been scalded.

'Don't worry, Damian!' she exclaimed with withering bitterness. 'I've never cherished any false hopes of it being reciprocated or anything as foolish as that. In fact I realised from the start that it was the second biggest mistake of my life.'

'And the first?'

'I'd have hoped you'd realise that was in ever coming to Ireland at all.'

'You hope too much,' he stated with chilling softness. 'You seem to forget that the only thing I understand about you is your body.'

He reached out and began slowly undoing the buttons of her shirt. Rosanne's eyes lowered to those strong, tanned hands against her, then closed tightly. Yet it was as though she still saw those hands, her bemused mind mesmerised by the deft precision with which they worked.

'But if, as you claim, you love me,' he continued in those same chillingly soft tones, 'you'll understand and accept that tonight, above all nights, is one that I need to spend in the oblivion of your arms.'

Her eyes remained tightly shut as he slowly stripped every article of clothing from her body. Motionless, her every effort was directed at remaining in control as she forced herself to face that what he was doing was using her in the most humiliating manner he possibly could. But there was no respite from the delicate sureness of those hands as they moved methodically from one garment to the next, their feather-light touch inflaming her to a pitch of need that brought silent shrieks of protest clamouring in her head.

It was only when she stood naked before him that he shrugged out of his heavy overcoat, then took her unresisting hands and placed them against his chest.

'Take all the time you like undressing me,' he said, a hint of hoarseness warming the chill drawl of his words, 'while I feast my eyes on your beauty. And, whatever else you may be, you are a most beautiful woman, Ros...anne.'

They both momentarily froze as the telephone rang. Then they were racing one another in panic to reach it, his long legs winning over hers as he lifted the receiver and barked his name into it.

'Yes...yes,' he muttered, while Rosanne, oblivious of her nakedness, pressed herself impatiently against him as she tried to bring her ear within reach of the receiver. 'Right—we'll be there in the morning. And thanks for letting me know.'

'Know what?' she almost screamed at him as he replaced the receiver.

'She's out of the coma and sleeping peacefully,' he said in a hollow, oddly detached voice. 'She wants to see us both in the morning.'

The words were scarcely out of him when, as he reached for her, his tall frame stooped suddenly as he buried his head against the curve of her neck and sobbed like a child.

She folded her arms tenderly around those broad, heaving shoulders, her own tears of relief coursing unnoticed down her face as she rested her cheek against his head.

'Oh, Damian, I——'

'No!' he choked in angry protest. 'There's nothing you can say—so don't even try!'

'Perhaps you're right,' she whispered sadly, clasping him even tighter. 'But I'm saying it anyway... because I want you to know that I'm here if you need me.'

'Well, I don't!' he raged, lifting his head and gazing down at her from eyes ravaged with anguish and bitterness. Then, with a soft growl of protest, he crushed her in his arms, his lips inflicting fevered, biting kisses on her face and mouth while over and over, as though trying to convince himself, he kept chanting, 'I don't need you... I don't need you.'

He lifted her in his arms and carried her to his room, then he lowered her to her feet and began tearing his own clothes from him. Yet, despite his chanted denials, the rage of need in him simply to hold her was such that he kept breaking off from his frantic stripping of himself to hold her against him in a desperate, almost suffocating embrace.

It was his determination to keep her in his arms, while at the same time tearing himself free of the last of his clothing, that landed them in a feverishly entwined heap on the velvety thickness of the clothes-strewn carpet.

And it was there that passion overpowered them, swift and violent in the devastating urgency of its need, yet mercifully sweet in the total oblivion into which its driving turbulence hurled them. As though locked in mortal battle, each made increasingly wilder and impossibly excessive demands of the other as though searching for a limit. But as each impossible demand was answered with reckless totality a truce was finally imposed on their passionate warring as their glistening bodies clung together as though in mutual protection from the explosive force raging through them.

Though no word passed between them, as they lay locked and trembling in one another's arms, it was a silence born of a fulfilment so complete that it lulled them into the protective shelter of sleep before reality had any chance to begin eroding its completeness.

Rosanne awoke later as she felt him lift her from the floor to the bed. There was a gentleness in his hands as he drew the covers around them, but it was a coldness emanating from deep within her that made her reach out to him, her shivering body clinging and entwining itself around his as it desperately sought his warmth.

But it was the heat swiftly trembling from her to which his own body eventually responded, and it was her instinctive awareness of his momentary reluctance that brought the wildness of desperation to her response to the unfamiliar gentleness with which he began making love to her.

Later, when once again lost in the explosive turbulence of passion, she cried out her love, but received no sign that he had even heard her incautious words.

'Damian, we can't go on like this,' pleaded Rosanne, as they sped their way to the clinic.

'Like what?'

With angry despair, she glanced sharply at the grim profile of the man at the wheel, her heart constricting painfully as she did so. He looked ghastly, she thought anxiously—and shaving had done little to remove that look of ravaged desperation from his face.

'Acting as though I don't exist,' she sighed in reply. 'You've barely spoken more than a couple of——'

'That's probably because I'd feel a good deal better if you didn't exist,' he cut in harshly. 'And as for conversation, I'd have thought last night would have made it perfectly clear that conversation was the least of my interests in you.'

Recoiling from the callous brutality of that statement, Rosanne felt bitter anger rising in her as she found herself automatically trying to excuse him. But there was no excuse for such obvious and deliberate cruelty, she told herself angrily—no matter what he was suffering. And neither was there any excuse for an allegedly intelligent person such as herself to be convinced that she would spend the rest of her life pining for such a callous monster. He didn't deserve love—not hers nor that of any other sane woman!

'As you've been so refreshingly frank,' she replied icily, doggedly steering her mind away from its sudden pre-occupation with the idea that she might no longer actually be technically sane, 'perhaps you won't object if I'm equally so. And, to be perfectly frank, I couldn't give a damn if we never exchanged another word. But I suggest, and solely for Hester's sake, that we at least try to be civil to one another in her presence—though perhaps that's too much to ask of someone as grossly arrogant and self-centred as you are,' she finished off with bitter disgust, as what little control she had managed to dredge up began deserting her completely.

'Arrogant and self-centred?' he mocked. 'And they told me love was blind.'

'Perhaps they should also have told you that the line between love and hate can be so fine as to be almost indistinguishable,' Rosanne hurled at him with loathing.

His only reply was a cynically dismissive laugh as he swung the car into a parking space, then he turned towards her, his expression grimly implacable.

'As you know, they've only been letting her have one visitor at a time,' he stated coldly. 'But in the unlikely event of our being allowed in together we'll not only be civil in her presence, we'll be any damned thing she wants us to be—understood?'

Without giving her a chance to reply, he leapt from the car and began striding, two at a time, up the entrance steps, turning as he reached the top and waiting with frowning impatience for her to catch up with him.

They weren't allowed in together, and it was Damian who Hester had made it known she wanted to see first.

As she began her long wait, Rosanne found herself thinking of that special love between Damian and Hester that had struck her from the start. Though she had envied them that easygoing, bickering love, she hadn't begrudged them it, she thought sadly—it was just that, having witnessed it, she couldn't help but wonder what sort of similarly beautiful relationship might have developed between herself and her grandmother had it ever had the chance.

When Damian finally emerged, he looked pale and spent.

'She wants to see you now, Rosanne,' he told her quietly.

She rose and went to her grandmother's room, the thought suddenly striking her that he had just addressed her by her true name—and for the first time had done so with no trace of sarcastic emphasis in his tone.

It was as though the tiny figure, now almost lost in the huge, starched whiteness of the hospital bed, had shrunk overnight. But as Rosanne leaned over and tenderly kissed her grandmother's cheek she felt hope career dizzily through her as she momentarily glimpsed the familiar teasing twinkle dance in those faded eyes.

'Sit yourself down, my darling—there are so many things we still have to say to one another.'

Rosanne drew up a chair as close as she could to the bed, then sat down, leaning forward and clasping one of Hester's hands in hers as she tried desperately not to give any sign of the anguish that had filled her on hearing the fading strength in those whispered words.

'I've sorted out with Damian what I want him to do and I feel a lot better for it,' whispered Hester. 'But you and I have been cheated of so much . . . I keep remembering things I should have told you yesterday. I didn't tell you about Paul...your father. Although he knew from your mother that my heart was always with them...I always felt he must have had his doubts. Faith rang me from the airport before she and Paul took off on that last...'

'It's all right,' choked Rosanne as her grandmother's voice broke, 'you mustn't upset yourself.'

'What would upset me would be for you not to know that your father and I had a long talk...I've always thanked God I was given that one chance to reassure and be reassured...and it's something I had to pass on to you, my darling.'

'I'm so glad...so glad,' whispered Rosanne, tears streaming down her cheeks.

If only her father had had a chance to tell his own father, she thought sadly, clinging to her grandmother's hands as all the 'if onlys' crowded in torment into her mind.

As they had the previous day, they exchanged the small confidences each knew the other would derive joy from, but now there was an added urgency in those exchanges and its presence filled Rosanne's heart with a sharp terror.

'I want my darling boy with me!' Hester suddenly exclaimed. 'Where is he?'

Rosanne flew to the door and even before she had it fully opened Damian had risen and was racing towards her.

'She's asking for you,' she choked, her heart going out to him as she saw him check his frantic stride to an almost leisurely pace as he walked past her into the room.

'I'm here, Hessie,' he whispered, sitting on the edge of the bed, his large, strong hands dwarfing the tiny one he gathered between them.

Rosanne returned to her seat, lifting her grandmother's free hand and pressing it gently to her cheek.

She heard the door open and then the soft murmur of voices in the background, but her eyes were closed as she clung in prayer to that fragile hand.

'You, my darling Damian, have been secure in the knowledge of my love for you almost from the moment you were born ... though that doesn't go to say I'm prepared to take much of the blame for the wicked young devil you've turned out to be ... I've a feeling you've always known it was the devil in you that was one of the things I've so loved about you.' Despite their disjointed slowness, the teasing indulgence in those words managed to shine through. 'Whereas Rosanne has been denied all those carefree years you and I shared ... and with them the almost arrogant confidence that comes with knowing what it is to be loved without question. But you too have my love, my darling Rosanne, and the fact it has been for so short a time in no way lessens its depth.'

A still, expectant silence seemed to hover in the room— one which neither man nor girl seemed able to dispel.

'And now, at the risk of sounding a sentimental old fool,' whispered Hester, the words now struggling from her, 'I'd like to tell you what joy it brings me to have the two people I love most here with me now. But there's one thing I must ask you.'

'What?' both croaked out in unison.

'Would you, for God's sake, take those doleful expressions off your faces? The pair of you are worse than a week of wet Sundays!'

'Counsel her!' exploded Damian in reply to the murmured words of condolence offered by one of the group of medical staff who had gathered around them. 'She might need it,' he snarled, casting a bitter, accusing look at Rosanne, 'but I don't!'

'Try not to take it too personally,' one of the doctors reassured Rosanne, placing a comforting arm around her shoulder. 'Grief can do terrible things to people—and they lash out at those closest to them.'

Rosanne tore herself free and raced out after Damian. 'Damian!'

He swung round, his expression blank as he faced her. 'I'll take you to the Fogartys',' he muttered expressionlessly. 'Hester will be buried from home...Hank and Rosanne can bring you up when the time comes.'

And those, apart from a few courtesy exchanges later enforced on him in the harrowing days that followed, were the last words he ever exchanged with her.

CHAPTER ELEVEN

'DARLING, were your ears burning? Hank and I were just discussing the fact that it's about time you came over to see us.'

Rosanne felt that now-familiar mixture of pleasure and pain that assailed her whenever she heard the cheery, lilting voice of her mother's closest friend.

'Once I've caught up on all the things I have to do here, I'll be over—I promise,' she hedged lightly, her mind suddenly veering back to their first meeting.

'My God—how could anyone ever have missed it?' Rosanne Fogarty had exclaimed, flinging her arms around her namesake and hugging her tightly. 'You're a perfect blend of Faith and Paul!'

The rapport between them had been instant and total, and it had been Rosanne and her husband, Hank, whose loving strength had supported her during those terrible days following her grandmother's death. They had remained in regular contact over the telephone since her return to England, but the pleasure of hearing either of their voices was always tainted by the memories evoked of Ireland—that broodingly beautiful, intoxicatingly enchanting land of mountains and mystery which had become inseparable from Damian in her tortured heart.

'Well, don't leave it too long,' pleaded Rosanne Fogarty, 'or you'll have the boys to answer to. The other day they actually went as far as to say that, for a girl, you were OK. And you know my sons, darling—that's as close to a declaration of love you'll get from either of them!'

'How are they?' Rosanne chuckled—Michael and Paul, the Fogartys' fourteen-year-old twins, were the most delightful pair of rascals she had ever come across.

'They've both had miserable colds. Is the weather still as bad with you as it is with us?'

Rosanne glanced through the latticed windows of the cottage that had once been her grandfather's home, and was now hers.

'It's terrible,' she sighed, feeling as unsettled as the abysmal weather. 'It's decided to rain now, but it was hailing down golf balls half an hour ago.'

'It's been like that up in Donegal, according to Damian.' The Irish woman hesitated, then continued. 'We all met up the other day for the reading of Hester's will. Darling, that's one of the things I wanted to talk to you about. She left me some of her jewellery, but she made that will before she found you. I want you to have it.'

'No,' protested Rosanne, her eyes filling with tears— as they unaccountably kept doing of late. 'Perhaps I could have a small memento of her, but——'

'Darling, there are one or two things I must insist you have—but we'll not argue about it now,' cut in the older woman gently. 'I also meant to tell you I ran into Cedric Lamont—he said to thank you for all the bumph you'd sent off to him and that he'd like to meet you when you're over. I hadn't realised you'd actually finished off those notes, darling.'

'It was what Hester would have wanted,' replied Rosanne unsteadily, battling to suppress the memories welling up in her of that last, desolate day she had spent in Sheridan Hall. 'Rosanne, all I need is a little more time,' she choked. 'And I promise I'll be back to see you.'

'I understand, darling,' replied Rosanne Fogarty quietly. 'It wasn't a subject I felt it appropriate to bring up when we were last together... but I do understand.'

Rosanne felt as though she was cutting herself off from the only warmth left in her life as she replaced the receiver. She gazed around her, her heart filling with bitter resentment that it was now so obsessed by the memory of one man that even here, in the home she had once so loved, she was unable to find any peace.

She started as the doorbell rang, then rubbed her hands almost reflexly against her cheeks as she went to answer the door—several people had recently remarked on how pale she looked.

In the few seconds it had taken him to get from what Bridie had always referred to as 'that fancy Italian car' to the door the rain had soaked him.

'This is almost as bad as Ireland!' exclaimed Damian Sheridan, his casually conversational words at complete odds with the hooded wariness of his eyes.

'Damian?' Rosanne was still croaking out his name as he strode past her and into the hall that seemed suddenly to shrink with his size.

'Let me take your coat,' she offered stiltedly, her mouth suddenly so dry that she had difficulty forming the words.

He deposited a leather attaché case at his feet, then shrugged out of his coat and handed it to her.

'You don't seem exactly surprised to see me,' he observed in those familiar, drawling tones of his while his eyes took their disconcertingly candid stock of her.

Possibly because he was so constantly and vividly in her thoughts that seeing him here in the flesh made little difference, she told herself, her mind in a peculiarly detached daze as she hung up his coat.

It was only when she turned and faced him once more that the shock of his presence belatedly hit her and she felt herself swaying back heavily against the damp coat she had just hung up, her legs crumpling beneath her.

'I'm sorry,' he whispered hoarsely, reaching out a hand to steady her. 'I thought of ringing—then decided against it.'

'Why?' she croaked, her mind disintegrating into turmoil.

He hesitated, then gave a slightly sheepish grin. It was that grin that destroyed her. Until that moment there had been only shock—now there was love, unleashed and rampaging in desperate yearning throughout her.

'I didn't ring because I decided the odds were you'd hang up on me.' He pulled a small face, glancing around him. 'Is there somewhere we could sit—or don't you plan on letting me any further than the hall?'

'I...I'm sorry,' she mumbled, reflex politeness dictating her words and guiding her to lead him through to the living-room, despite the fact that she had no idea if her legs would carry her that far. 'Would you like some tea?' she asked, still on automatic pilot. 'Or perhaps a whiskey or brandy—you're wet and you must be cold.'

'I don't want anything,' he replied ungraciously, flinging himself down on the worn leather chair that had been her grandfather's favourite. He scowled up at her as she remained standing. 'Stop being so damned hostessy and sit down, will you? You're making me feel nervous.'

'Since when did you ever feel nervous?' exploded Rosanne, all the old anger and resentment that was almost forgotten erupting swiftly within her.

'On that fulsome note of welcome, I suppose we might as well get down to business,' he drawled, reaching for the case he had brought in with him as Rosanne flung herself down on the sofa.

'You and I have no business,' she informed him, trying without success to ignore the exhilarating feeling pulsating through her of once more being completely alive. The past few weeks had been empty and soulless, she realised with mounting despair, and now it was as though she had been regenerated.

'I'd not be here if we hadn't,' he contradicted brusquely, opening the case and removing a sheaf of papers. 'Hester had no time to change her will, so she asked me to carry out her final wishes.'

Rosanne gave him a startled look.

'I don't see how that should affect me,' she muttered warily. 'She gave me all I ever wanted of her,' she added, steeling herself against the tears yet again threatening her and vowing to herself that she would see a doctor—it couldn't possibly be normal.

'What the hell's that supposed to mean?' he demanded angrily. 'Don't Hester's wishes count?'

'Of course they count,' she protested tearfully—why did he always have to tie her up in knots like this? 'All I meant was that I wanted nothing more than her acceptance of who I was...and her love.'

'But the fact is that she was a considerably wealthy woman.'

'Can't you understand? I've no interest in her wealth or possessions!'

'Whether you're interested or not, they exist,' he pointed out sharply. 'Not so much possessions—she didn't go in for those much—but the wealth is, as I've said, considerable.'

'Who did she leave it to in her will?'

'To me, of course——'

'Well, keep it!' Rosanne flung at him angrily. 'I neither want it nor need it. My grandfather left me all I'll ever need.'

'I'm perfectly aware that Edward Bryant left you exceptionally well provided for. I had you thoroughly checked out,' he stated quietly. 'But that has no bearing whatever on Hester's wishes.'

Rosanne barely heard those last words as she gazed across at him in wide-eyed horror. 'You had me checked out? Are you...? You can't possibly have thought——'

'I thought you might have blown your job,' he interrupted her disjointed stammerings impatiently, 'or that recent happenings might have left you with no stomach for it. For all I knew, your salary was all you had to live on. I could hardly let you starve when there was all Hester's money there—now could I? That's why I had to have you checked out.'

'It was kind of you,' whispered Rosanne, feeling almost sick with relief that he hadn't actually suspected she had been a fraud, even though she was perfectly aware that it was probably one of the most ridiculous fears she had ever had. 'But surely you can see that I simply don't need any more than I already have.'

'And surely *you* can see that *I* most certainly don't,' he retorted with weary impatience. 'Rosanne, there's always been far more money than sense in the Sheridan family, and I was born with an over-abundance of it...the money, I mean.'

Rosanne's eyes met his, then dropped as, instead of the familiar, teasing laughter they had sought, they found only guarded tension.

'Anyway, it's what Hester wants that counts—so I've had the lot made over to you.'

'Are you saying that's what she asked you to do—give me all and you nothing?' asked Rosanne disbelievingly.

'Well, no...she mentioned something about half, but——'

'You're the one who said it's her wishes that count,' she pointed out, 'so why aren't you carrying them out?'

'Damn it—do you have to split hairs?' he roared. 'I've had my lawyers and accountants tearing their hair out over this for days—the tax side of it was murderously complicated—so I'm not going back to them to ask them to start all over again with another sum! To start talking in terms of splitting things down the middle is crazy. There's the jewellery to consider—and getting that lot valued would be a nightmare.'

'But she left her jewellery to Rosanne Fogarty,' she blurted out in bemusement. 'She was on the telephone to me only moments ago—saying she wanted me to have it.'

'What she left Rosanne wasn't the family stuff,' muttered Damian. 'Some of these pieces have been in the family for generations. Hester left them to me, presumably for any wife of mine to wear. I want you to have them.'

'Well, I suggest you find yourself a wife to wear them,' lashed out Rosanne blindly, the life she had felt surging through her now slowly draining from her as though in anticipation of his inevitable departure.

'OK—marry me,' he drawled, depositing the case on the floor then leaning back in the chair, his eyes challenging.

Rosanne got to her feet. 'I think it's best if you go now,' she said quietly, 'before we both...before I say things I might regret.'

He rose and walked over to her.

'Do you honestly believe I'm incapable of regretting the things I say?' he asked huskily. 'Do you think I haven't lain awake at night, cursing myself for all——?' He broke off with a groan and swept her into his arms. 'Rosanne, she had such hopes for us,' he whispered brokenly against her hair.

'No!' she protested, dragging herself from the only place she wanted to be, her head shaking vehemently.

She had always loved him for himself alone—but his interest in her, despite the powerful attraction between them from the start, had always seemed to be governed by Hester's wishes... he had once admitted as much to her.

'Damian, you always said you never knew me—but how could you?' she blurted out agitatedly. 'I couldn't be myself in Ireland... not when the real me would have been sickened by the terrible thing I was contemplating——' She broke off, shaking her head distractedly. 'No—that makes it sound as though I knew what I was doing, and I didn't! I was so warped by bitterness... I——' She couldn't finish, trying to choke back the tears.

'Rosanne, sit down,' he urged gently, guiding her, then sitting down beside her on the sofa.

'The most terrible thing about it all was that right from the start I knew Hester couldn't have had anything to do with my adoption,' she choked, tears streaming down her face. 'But that other person I'd become kept refusing to accept it!'

'It seems that the pair of strangers who met all those weeks ago were not only strangers to one another, but also to themselves,' sighed Damian, a peculiarly tentative smile creeping to his lips as he read the questioning suspicion in her eyes. 'Rosanne, when my parents were killed, I regarded a shock such as that as being just about the most devastating thing anyone, man or child, could be asked to face. It took a long time, but I coped...and that was because I had Hester. But when she told me her illness was terminal...that I found impossible to face. I can't even begin to describe what knowing that did to me...I felt driven to try to squeeze every last second out of every day I had left with her. To me it seemed to be that much less bearable than my parents' death. With Hester I knew the crippling sense of loss that was to come, just as it had with them...but with her it was the devastation that came with the anticipation of losing her that I found impossible to handle.

'She sensed what I was going through and did everything in her power to help me,' he raced on as though unable to stop. 'She used to tease me—threatening to send out for a caseload of cotton wool for me to wrap her in. Rosanne, it was that smothering, tortured creature that you had the misfortune to meet those weeks ago...that's why I speak of us as strangers even to ourselves.'

Rosanne knew it was the wrong thing to do, but the love in her was too strong for her to have any thought of the consequences as she put her arms around him. He did what she least expected, drawing back from her instantly.

'No,' he muttered, shaking his head as he gave a bitter laugh. 'As Hester would say—I always was the perverse devil,' he added confusingly, then began gazing round the room with an air that seemed suspiciously close to boredom to Rosanne, who was now feeling like a wrung-out rag.

'I was only offering you a bit of sympathy, for heaven's sake,' she snapped, thoroughly disconcerted. 'I can't see what all the fuss is about!'

'Who's making a fuss?' he drawled, flashing her an almost malevolent look. 'And besides, we both know where your offers of sympathy had led in the past.'

'In the past—precisely!' she ground out, horrified by those taunting words. 'Because it's my sympathy—and that alone—which is on offer now!'

'I preferred it when it was the rest of you on offer as well,' he stated in such matter-of-fact tones that for a moment Rosanne wondered if she had heard the words correctly.

'Well, that's your problem,' she snapped, deciding this could only be some warped form of joke.

'So—I didn't turn out to be the love of your life after all.' He sighed theatrically.

'Damian, you may find this terribly amusing,' she said, hurt beyond measure to realise that, far from there being any shred of understanding or forgiveness in him, he had come here simply to torment and humiliate her, 'but I'm afraid I don't.'

'You're mistaken if you think I find this amusing, Rosanne,' he stated curtly. 'You know how terrified I am by the tales of how single-mindedly a Sheridan falls in love, and you, after all, have Sheridan blood in you... Doesn't what lies in store for you terrify the living daylights out of you?'

'You'll never forgive me, will you?' she protested hoarsely, barely able to believe that he was doing this to her. 'You were so driven by your desperation to do whatever Hester wanted that you even got yourself involved with me. Don't her wishes matter now that she's no longer with us? Because what she wanted most was that you'd be able to understand or, failing that, at least find it in your heart to forgive me what I did . . . and that you just can't bring yourself to do!'

'Rosanne, why the hell do you have to be so selective in your memory of things I've said?' he demanded wearily. 'You seem to have forgotten one of the more rational things I said—that nobody leads me anywhere I don't want to go, and that included Hester!' He dragged his hands over his face in a gesture of exhaustion. 'Of course I understand what must have driven you. God almighty, if George Cranleigh had been alive when I learned what he'd done—and not least of all to you— he'd have been six feet under in no time unless someone had the sense to put me in a strait-jacket. As for for- giving—Rosanne, you're the one I should be asking for- giveness of.' Without looking at her, he reached out and took her hand in his. 'And I'm asking for it—can you ever forgive me, Rosanne?'

'Of course I do,' she whispered almost automatically, as her stunned mind tried vainly to catch up with this complete turn-about.

'You must have realised I could have got my lawyers to put those papers in the post, rather than my coming here,' he said quietly.

Rosanne glanced down at the documents on the floor, the bemused strugglings of her mind not in the least aided by the insidious heat radiating through her from the hand still holding hers.

'I've thought a lot about the terrible strain you must have been under,' he continued. 'And, knowing how ir- rationally I'd behaved under pressure, I tried to work out how it might have affected you. Imagining yourself to be in love with me, I decided, was probably an odds- on certainty.' He lifted her hand and seemed to examine it momentarily, then lowered it once more—still wrapped in his. 'Odds-on certainties, of course, have been known to lose on the rare occasion,' he muttered. 'But when I asked you to marry me—you told me to leave. When I took you in my arms—you turned away and said no. And when——'

'Hold on a moment,' protested Rosanne weakly, her mind, even in its present state of completed befuddlement, detecting a blatant manipulation of the facts. 'Damian, you're twisting everything! You didn't ask me to marry you——'

'I said the words!'

'Yes, but——'

'And if you'd loved me as only a Sheridan can, you'd have leapt at any proposal, no matter how it was worded,' he muttered almost accusingly.

Rosanne twisted round in order to see his face clearly. What she saw was a mutinous scowl.

'Are you completely out of your mind?' she almost squeaked. If she lived to be a hundred she would never understand him!

'Yes.'

'Damian...oh, for heaven's sake, I give up!' she groaned. What was the point trying to have a conversation with a self-confessed madman?

'Do you remember the first day we met?' he demanded.

'Yes,' she whispered, startled out of her exasperation by the sudden rush of memories that his unexpected question evoked.

'I said you reminded me of someone.'

'Yes,' she replied, her growing suspicion that he wasn't entirely sane overriding the effect of those memories.

'I said it would come to me who it was—and it did.'

And now he was going to tell her she was a dead ringer for his aunt Mildred or someone, she told herself edgily.

'It was a nightmare I used to have.'

It took a couple of seconds for his words to sink in.

'Thanks a million, Damian,' she said warily, loath to look at him for fear that he might actually look as unbalanced as he sounded.

'Not that there were actual features, or anything, of the girl in my nightmare,' he continued. 'I was only a kid when I had it.'

'It must have been a really awful nightmare,' she murmured, horrified to find that she was having difficulty keeping her face straight—after all, this was the man she was doomed to love for the rest of her life!

'Stop being so damned patronising!' he rounded on her. 'If you must know, I had that nightmare after listening to them all prattling on about that wretched old wives' tale about the Sheridans in love...people should think twice before coming out with that sort of thing with kids around!' he exclaimed indignantly. 'Anyway, I realised that you were very likely the one it was going to happen to me with.'

Rosanne thought long and hard over that tortuous sentence, and still it remained unintelligible.

'I beg your pardon?' she managed eventually.

'I knew I was probably going to fall in love with you,' he paraphrased, not attempting to hide his impatience. 'And far worse than any nightmare it turned out to be— I can tell you.'

'But I dare say you'll manage to describe it in all its gory detail,' croaked Rosanne, the words slurring in her ears as her head began swimming terrifyingly.

'There's no call for sarcasm,' he snapped. 'You...Rosanne? Are you all right?' he exclaimed anxiously.

'Of course I'm not all right!' she wailed. 'I've been sitting here for the last few minutes, convinced I've been talking to a raving lunatic! Damian, have you by any chance just told me you love me?'

'I thought I'd made it perfectly clear.' He sounded almost offended.

'Damian, I could kill you! I could...please, just put your arms around me,' she begged disjointedly as her mind, having carried out a careful sifting through of his words, decided that he had made himself, if not perfectly, at least relatively clear.

'No.'

'Why not?' she demanded, having once again sifted through his words.

'Because...we'll just end up... Damn it, Rosanne, you know where we'll end up!'

'Damian, we were both under the most dreadful pressure when we met,' she stated patiently, ignoring the baleful look he gave her as she tucked her legs under her and knelt beside him on the sofa.

'So?' he growled uncooperatively.

'Yet, despite the terrible strain you were under, your worst nightmare really did come true.'

'At the risk of sounding repetitive,' he growled with even less co-operation, 'so?'

'So did mine.' She gave a disbelieving groan as he looked at her blankly. 'Or—to put it another way—the odds-on favourite lost.'

'Would you mind putting your arms around me and repeating that?' he asked, his voice not in the least steady.

She flung her arms around him. 'I love you! I love you!' she cried.

'Thank God for that,' he groaned, resting his head against hers as his arms tightened fiercely around her. 'Something tells me this nightmare of ours has just turned into the most beautiful of dreams...oh, Rosanne, I love you.'

'Why couldn't you have said so when I told you I loved you?' she protested, burying her face against his neck and drinking in the sweet, familiar scent of his skin.

'How could I when, no matter how much I loved you, I could make neither head nor tail of you?' he protested, his mouth seeking out hers. 'But now nothing's ever going to stop this perfect dream from becoming our reality,' he vowed fiercely. 'Rosanne, have you any idea how much I love you?'

'If it's anything like as much as I love you, there aren't words enough to describe it,' she choked, happiness lurching through her in drunken chaos.

'That's exactly how much,' he whispered contentedly. 'And that's the way it's always going to be. Which reminds me—when I left today, Bridie gave me one of her most crabbit looks and informed me it was about time I went off to find you and bring you back home...and that's all I want from life—for you to come home with me and be my wife. Will you?'

'Yes, oh, yes!' she choked, laughing and crying and bursting with an indescribable joy. 'And it *will* be going home—I've been so homesick...for the house, for Bridie and James, for——'

'Don't I feature anywhere in all this?' he growled softly, his lips nuzzling hungrily against hers.

'You feature everywhere in everything,' she whispered huskily, a shiver rippling through her as his hands embarked on some very serious trespassing, 'because you are my life.'

He drew slightly back from her, love hot and dark in his eyes. 'And you mine...now and forever.' He lowered his head to hers, his mouth hungry and impatient on hers. 'I know we still have a thousand things to say to one another,' he breathed urgently against her lips. 'But as we have the rest of our lives in which to say them . . . would you mind very much if we left them just a little while longer?'

She gave him her reply in passionate and total silence—and he understood every word of it.

Coming Next Month

HARLEQUIN PRESENTS®

#1773 LOVE'S PRISONER Elizabeth Oldfield
Piers Armstrong was a newly released hostage—and Suzy
wanted to feature him in her new book. But, after all that
had happened between them three years ago, would Piers
want to do Suzy any favors?

#1774 YESTERDAY'S ECHOES Penny Jordan
Rosie had been seduced at a party when she was a
teenager—and Jake Lucas seemed to know all her secrets.
Would he despise her for them and shatter the fragile peace
she'd fought hard to create in her life?

#1775 NEVER A BRIDE Diana Hamilton (Wedlocked!)
Clare and Jake's marriage was a paper one, based on convenience. Only now Clare had foolishly fallen in love
with her husband!

#1776 SLAVE TO LOVE Michelle Reid
Roberta finally realized she'd never be more than
Soloman Maclaine's mistress. She had to leave—could she
give up their sweet nights of passion?

#1777 HOT NOVEMBER Ann Charlton (Dangerous Liaisons)
Matt MacKenzie had warned Emma that it only took one
spark to start a blaze—and there were bushfires everywhere!
November was going to be a very hot month indeed...in
every sense!

#1778 SCANDALS & SECRETS Miranda Lee
(Book 5 of Hearts of Fire)
The fifth in a compelling six-part saga—discover the passion,
scandal, sin and hope that exist between two fabulously rich
families.

Celeste Campbell had lived on her hatred of Byron Whitmore
for twenty years—and revenge was sweet. But suddenly
Celeste found she could no longer deny her long-buried
feelings of desire for Byron.... Meanwhile, Gemma realized
exactly how much she cared for Nathan—when she heard
him talking to his ex-wife, Lenore, as if they were lovers!

MILLION DOLLAR SWEEPSTAKES (III)

No purchase necessary. To enter, follow the directions published. Method of entry may vary. For eligibility, entries must be received no later than March 31, 1996. No liability is assumed for printing errors, lost, late or misdirected entries. Odds of winning are determined by the number of eligible entries distributed and received. Prizewinners will be determined no later than June 30, 1996.

Sweepstakes open to residents of the U.S. (except Puerto Rico), Canada, Europe and Taiwan who are 18 years of age or older. All applicable laws and regulations apply. Sweepstakes offer void wherever prohibited by law. Values of all prizes are in U.S. currency. This sweepstakes is presented by Torstar Corp., its subsidiaries and affiliates, in conjunction with book, merchandise and/or product offerings. For a copy of the Official Rules send a self-addressed, stamped envelope (WA residents need not affix return postage) to: MILLION DOLLAR SWEEPSTAKES (III) Rules, P.O. Box 4573, Blair, NE 68009, USA.

EXTRA BONUS PRIZE DRAWING

No purchase necessary. The Extra Bonus Prize will be awarded in a random drawing to be conducted no later than 5/30/96 from among all entries received. To qualify, entries must be received by 3/31/96 and comply with published directions. Drawing open to residents of the U.S. (except Puerto Rico), Canada, Europe and Taiwan who are 18 years of age or older. All applicable laws and regulations apply; offer void wherever prohibited by law. Odds of winning are dependent upon number of eligibile entries received. Prize is valued in U.S. currency. The offer is presented by Torstar Corp., its subsidiaries and affiliates in conjunction with book, merchandise and/or product offering. For a copy of the Official Rules governing this sweepstakes, send a self-addressed, stamped envelope (WA residents need not affix return postage) to: Extra Bonus Prize Drawing Rules, P.O. Box 4590, Blair, NE 68009, USA.

SWP-H1095

HARLEQUIN  PRESENTS®

Don't be late for the wedding!

Be sure to make a date in your diary for the happy event.

The fourth in our tantalizing new selection of stories...

Wedlocked!

Bonded in matrimony, torn by desire...

Watch for:

Never a Bride by Diana Hamilton
(Harlequin Presents #1775)

"Diana Hamilton stirs up the sparks..."
—*Romantic Times*

What do you do if you're a woman capable of strong
passions and emotions, and you fall in love with a man
who doesn't want you? And what do you do when that man
is your husband...in name only? Clare and Jake's marriage
had been one of convenience: could it ever become a
true romance?

Available in November, wherever Harlequin books are sold

Become a Privileged Woman,

You'll be entitled to all these *Free Benefits*. And *Free Gifts*, too.

To thank you for buying our books, we've designed an exclusive FREE program called *PAGES & PRIVILEGES™*. You can enroll with just one Proof of Purchase, and get the kind of luxuries that, until now, you could only read about.

BIG HOTEL DISCOUNTS

A privileged woman stays in the finest hotels. And so can you—at up to 60% off! Imagine standing in a hotel check-in line and watching as the guest in front of you pays $150 for the same room that's only costing you $60. Your *Pages & Privileges* discounts are good at Sheraton, Marriott, Best Western, Hyatt and thousands of other fine hotels all over the U.S., Canada and Europe.

FREE DISCOUNT TRAVEL SERVICE

A privileged woman is always jetting to romantic places. When you fly, just make one phone call for the lowest published airfare at time of booking— or double the difference back!

PLUS—you'll get a $25 voucher to use the first time you book a flight AND 5% cash back on every ticket you buy thereafter through the travel service!